A REVELATION

PATRICK J. WILLIAMS

Dedication

To the departed Rev Thomas M. Gillespie,

Oblates of Saint Francis de Sales:

You were a true man of faith who not only instructed his students, he inspired them. Thank you for encouraging my writing back when I was loaded with acne and finding my way as a struggling freshman at

Northeast Catholic High School for Boys, Philadelphia, PA

Contents

Chapter One

A Degenerate

Peach-soft light pressed against his eyelids, specks of brightness sifting through the dark. For a few fleeting seconds, everything was still and silent.

As morning broke, a happy sound filled the air—the loud, rhythmic purring of a faithful companion. Slowly, he opened his eyes in the loft, six feet above the ground. There, stretched out on his chest, was Jersey. The black cat stared at him patiently, her golden eyes unwavering, waiting for breakfast.

She was the velvet night woven into feline form, a creature born of gleam and shadow. Her coat, smooth as silk, shone in a deep midnight hue that seemed to drink in the light, each strand shimmering—cosmic. Her eyes glimmered like lanterns in the dark, glowing with quiet wisdom and playfulness, as if she withheld secrets.

Her movements were poetry in motion—graceful, fluid, and deliberate, as though time bent to her will. She leapt with the elegance of a whispered breeze, her presence a harmony of tranquility and power. When she rested, her body curled into a crescent, a silent symbol of peace. There was a softness about her, a comforting stillness like the faint hum of a lilt.

She carried the serenity of night in the gentle arch of her back, the tender flick of her tail. She reminded him that beauty resided in subtle forms, wrapped in the gentle elegance of a sweet black cat.

"Good morning, sweetheart," he murmured, his voice hoarse with sleep. He sighed heavily, staring blankly at the ceiling. Jersey meowed softly, yawning as she rubbed her face against his chest.

He stroked her fur gently, a faint smile pulling at the corners of his lips. "Keeping me company, huh?"

Now fully awake, the weight of the world was etched subtly into the lines of his jaw. His blonde hair, once a crown of carefree youth, fell in soft waves over his brow, tousled by sorrow. Hazel eyes, once bright, now held the private depth of someone who had loved and lost—flickering with the ghosts of moments gone.

His body, sculpted and strong, betrayed no sign of the unraveling beneath the surface. Muscles honed by discipline masked an ache no amount of strength could suppress. His heart, heavy and fractured, beat with a hushed desperation, longing for something he couldn't name—searching for peace in the aftermath of a love that once felt like home.

His thoughts wandered to recent memories; snapshots of late-night parties and shared laughter now tinged with heartbreak. Waking was like a Tandy reboot: ignorance, then the onslaught of two years that felt like a lifetime—crumbled.

Leaning closer to Jersey, he whispered, "You miss her too?" Long walks, sharing food, movie nights, togetherness—all gone now, just echoes remaining.

He looked every bit the disheveled college student burning the candle at both ends. Last night wasn't the first time he had let his emotions get the better of him. As usual, he had tried to calm himself, alcohol propped up as a remedy. Passing out was the inevitable result. He knew what they called him; the word followed him down hallways as he tried to transform himself into someone else.

The room was in complete disarray. Clothes slumped where they fell; a stained chair wore wrinkled tees like a cloak. Zeppelin posters curled at the corners, held by desperate thumbtacks. On the battered couch, notebooks and pens wove into the mess. The brass lamp cast a warm ellipse on the carpet. The shelves, laden with leather-bound volumes and dusty tomes, bore the history of fraternity brothers who had once inhabited this space; their memories burned into the carpet.

In the corner, on a narrow, wobbly table, sat a lava lamp. It danced with molten dreams, its liquid amber and ruby pools rising and falling in a slow, mesmerizing waltz. Like molten stars in a suspended night, the inviting glow pulsed softly, spilling light over the curves of its glass vessel. Wax blobs drifted apart and merged again in an intimate symphony of fluid motion—a living abstraction. Each shift brought calm, a fleeting metamorphosis that slowed time and faded the world outside into irrelevance.

He fell into a routine that had grown all too familiar. Grabbing a dark blue mouthwash container from among the empty beer bottles scattered about, he swished the liquid across his teeth without the intention of picking up a toothbrush. He spritzed glass cleaner onto his shirt liberally—paying special attention to the armpits—to mask the stale post-adolescent aroma, then settled on the couch.

The TV flickered on, playing cartoons meant for 8-year-olds, a perfect distraction to numb his thoughts. On the table in front of him sat last night's leftovers—Chinese takeout in sticky white containers. The food smelled good but was cold. Crumpled napkins, soy sauce packets, and spicy mustard surrounded textbooks and unfinished homework. He speared a piece of cold chicken with a fork, chewing absentmindedly as he stared at the screen.

His roommate, Matthew, entered the room. The once-lively friend he had known in their fraternity years now seemed more devastated with each passing day, weighed down by heartbreak.

Matthew had tried to console him with clichéd advice—"plenty of fish in the sea" and the like—but nothing connected or resonated. The emotional chaos stirred and was inescapable.

Matthew was an enigma, a friend who never quite made sense. From the moment they met, he had idolized him, seemingly without reason. He urged him to lead the house two years ago and acted as his fiercest defender. Matthew would lie in oncoming traffic for him, always singing his praises, even when he wasn't around. The admiration felt almost awkward, like an ill-fitting suit.

Despite being only recently out of his teenage years, Matthew exuded a blend of timeless wisdom and youthful energy. His chestnut brown hair fell effortlessly in layers, as though perpetually ruffled by a brisk autumn breeze. His deep, observant eyes, shifting between brown and contemplative green depending on the light, carried a constant glimmer of thought—always on the verge of something profound.

Matthew wore a slight, pensive smile, the kind that suggested he'd seen the world with all its raw edges and yet still believed in its beauty. He moved with calm assurance, not loud or boastful, but with the modest confidence of someone who understood the weight of words and the power of silence. His clothes were simple: vintage band tees paired with well-worn jeans; a cardigan draped across his shoulders like a cloak of reflection.

"Enough, snap out of this," Matthew said, a wry grin on his face as he took a long pull from his potent blunt.

"I'm fine," he replied flatly.

Matthew thumbed the TV volume down and plucked the fork from his hand.

"Yeah, you're fine," he said, sarcasm lighting his eyes. "I might take drastic measures. If you weren't covered in General Tso's sauce, I'd drag you to class myself."

"Stay or leave, your choice. I'm working through this the best I can," he muttered, sinking deeper into the stained couch and turning up the volume on the animated show blaring from the TV.

"Whatever," Matthew said with a shrug, his tone light but his concern clear. "Last night, man... you might be embarrassed right now if you remembered any of it. Did you black out again?"

"You're interrupting my breakfast," he shot back, slurping a cold noodle of lo mein through his lips. "I'm already running late. I'll catch you later, okay?"

Matthew didn't preach; he produced a screenshot. "I reinstated your econ lab—the deadline was last night." He said it like the weather.

He sighed heavily, the sound a mix of annoyance and resignation. The day had to start, whether he wanted it to or not.

Every other minute, vivid images of her flashed in his mind—happy moments, like photographs cascading in a torturous slideshow. The memories reminded him of what was gone, a cruel reminder that he was utterly alone. *But Matthew was right, moving forward delays the pain.*

Rushing to leave the dank room, he glanced down and noticed Jersey, his black cat, sitting silently beside an empty bowl. The sight stopped his heart for a beat. Kneeling, he took a moment to show her affection, stroking her soft fur and murmuring apologies. He poured food into her bowl, kissed her head, and whispered, "Sorry, honey," before hurrying out the door.

The fraternity house, a microcosm of connections and power dynamics, felt like a dying relic of American social experiments. Amidst its chaos, it had shaped him. Balancing the challenges of a rigorous curriculum with the responsibilities of being a past fraternity president had tested him in ways he hadn't imagined—a leader with a permanent beer in his hand.

The reflection flickered through his mind as he stepped into the lively second-floor hallway. Pledges, newly initiated members, and seasoned brothers collided in a chaotic mix of camaraderie, clashing personalities, and alcohol-induced antics. The mansion, ancient and enduring, had become their sardine tin of youth. It was a life he couldn't yet imagine leaving behind as graduation loomed.

The hallway was dimly lit, sunlight sneaking through the weathered window crevices, mocking the brothers who hadn't slept. He swung open his door, greeted by an eruption of laughter. His brethren were seated on the malt-soaked carpet, deeply engrossed in a competitive drinking game. They acknowledged him with drunken nods but remained focused on their enthralling match of throwing bottle caps into plastic cups.

On the staircase leading to the second floor, an all-too-familiar sight greeted him: a passed-out brother sprawled on the steps. He paused in the doorway, the scene almost poetic in its exaggerated portrayal of collegiate life. Disgust mingled with a begrudging admiration for his peers' resilience.

Amidst the chaos, Mark, his designated "little brother" in the hierarchy, called out to him. "You joining us? This game's getting intense. By the way, you've been wearing that same shirt for a week."

"Rain check," he replied, managing a broken smile. "I at least need to show my face in a class or two if I want to pass this year."

"Responsible as always," Mark teased, grinning. "Oh, by the way, about your cat."

"Yeah? What about her?" he asked, stifling a yawn.

"If we catch her wandering out of your room again," Mark warned with a mischievous grin, "we might have to... you know, take drastic measures."

"If this house were on fire, I'd let you all burn while saving that damn cat," he said, smirking as he played the role of a mock adversary. "Just a reminder—if you touch one strand of her fur."

"Noted," Mark replied with a chuckle. "Just keep her locked up during the 80s party tonight."

As he descended the stairs, he stepped casually over the brother unconsciously guarding the steps, treating the sight with the practiced nonchalance of someone who'd seen it all before. Just before reaching the ground floor, Mark called out again, still engrossed in the beer caps game.

"Before you go, any feedback for tonight's party?"

He paused, looking back with an expression that blended exasperation and humor. "Just make sure the music is legit 80s—not that early 90s mix-up like last year."

"Got it. No Vanilla Ice sneaking into the playlist this time," Mark replied with a grin.

"Just learn the difference between the 80s and early 90s. That's all I'm asking."

Mark laughed but quickly shifted gears, eager to share his plans. "We got these industrial-grade purple spotlights for the front of the house, like the kind they use at concerts!"

The mention of spotlights stopped him in his tracks. Halfway back up the stairs now, his past-president instincts kicked in, and he responded with a mix of sarcasm and genuine concern.

"Cool—until somebody catches a beam in their eyes and cracks a skull. You drunk morons. No spotlights." He heard himself sound like an old man and didn't care; the house still had his name on too many forms.

Mark, initially caught off guard by the abrupt shift in tone, pulled out his phone, clearly attempting to diffuse the situation.

The exchange ended with a subtle nod, but the camaraderie and weight of responsibility lingered in the air.

"Okay, calm down, dude. Look, here's what I made as my ringtone to go along with the theme tonight." His phone chimed the descending guitar of The Cure's *Just Like Heaven*. Two words—*show me*—and the air left his chest. The familiar strums resonated deep within him.

As the iconic melody filled the house, any hint of a smirk vanished from his face. The tune unearthed memories steeped in sadness, deepening the conflicted emotions swirling within him.

An abrupt, piercing vision of Lucia flooded his mind. He would never stop missing her; the chipped teal mug she hogged, steam ghosting her lip. The endless time loop continued, every step forward thwarted by a tidal wave of painful recollections. He clung to the past, his heart suspended in a void, uncertain whether light or darkness lay ahead.

Leaving the house more subdued than before, he passed through the grand, castle-like first floor and navigated past the impressive 250-year-old black wrought iron gate adorned with gothic designs. As was his habit, he turned slightly to admire his home of four years, noting its forthcoming farewell.

The front of the fraternity house stood like an ancient sentinel, its battered stone façade a tapestry of time, bearing the soft scars of centuries gone by. Ivy crept over its surface, tracing the building's edges, its tendrils curling around columns that rose like guards of forgotten lore. The black front door, heavy with oak and iron, loomed beneath an archway adorned with intricate carvings of faded symbols—each whispering secrets from initiations long past. Tall, narrow windows framed in ornate trim shimmered faintly in the light, as though bearing witness to generations of memories.

Above, the sloping roofline wore its hardened shingles like a badge of resilience, polished smooth by years of wind and rain. The house exuded a soundless dignity—not the flashy allure of modernity, but the steady confidence of something that had endured countless stories, laughter, and reflections etched into its stone.

He made his way down the street, initially heading toward his habitually neglected class. Upon reaching the academic building, he hesitated. Without much deliberation, he diverted toward the gym, opting to skip class again and find solace in a workout—a potential distraction from his inner turmoil. Or perhaps something deeper, something instinctual.

He often believed the best way to untangle mental knots was to prevent them from forming in the first place. Every decision, he mused, created a cascade of infinite possibilities that extended to our last days, leaving echoes that shaped others' lives. Briefly, he wondered about the path he would take if he attended class but quickly dismissed the thought, letting it dissipate.

The gym greeted him with its familiar atmosphere—a mix of humidity, pheromones, and the metallic clang of iron. He'd hoped the whispers were over. Last year's clip still lived online—bad angles, worse guesses. Stares followed him. Ignoring the chatter, he headed to the weight room, loading two 45-pound plates on either side of the bench press barbell—a ritualistic start to his workouts.

A group of young men approached.

"Are you that guy?" one asked directly.

He remained silent, focusing on his preparation.

"Is that all you can do or are you just warming up?" a third asked, genuinely curious.

He continued stretching, ignoring their persistent inquiries.

The young men exchanged glances, whispering among themselves.

Frustration bubbled beneath the surface as the murmurs grew louder. Without completing a single rep, he leapt to his feet and left the gym in a flash, his patience worn thin by the unwanted attention. He wouldn't feed the myth.

Determined to find relief, he decided to run, seeking solace in the rhythmic pounding of his footsteps and the challenge of pushing his body's limits. *She always wished he was in better shape. He found the discipline too late.* His endurance had grown remarkable in recent months; he could now maintain a brisk pace for nearly an hour without feeling drained.

Running had become a strange salvation—a counterbalance to the increased alcohol consumption that had taken hold since their division. With his headphones in, he set off from the West Philadelphia campus toward Center City, as had become custom. The sights of his classmates heading to lectures blurred and faded as he distanced himself from the university's boundaries, his focus turning inward with each step. Something was driving him.

He ran through neighborhoods as he had many times before, marveling at how the city could transform so drastically within just a few blocks. Philadelphia was a patchwork of extremes, a minefield, where areas notorious for crime nestled against affluent streets in a complex weave of wealth and poverty.

His route took him through a region inhabited by the impoverished, where individuals wandered aimlessly in a drug-induced haze, their presence casting a somber tint over the streets. Within moments, his long, measured strides carried him into a more well-off area. The air seemed lighter, the sidewalks lined with cheerful, prosperous people enjoying their lunches outdoors. The stark contrast between these two worlds never ceased to amaze.

Ahead, the towering skyline stretched toward the heavens, bathed in the soft glow of mid-afternoon sunlight that cast a golden hue along its edges. He passed cobblestone streets where the murmurs of the old world lingered in every crack, harmonizing with the aspirations of the new world rising ever higher.

The scent of fresh coffee from bustling cafes mingled with the earthy aroma of fallen leaves crunching underfoot. The air nipped, his breath slightly fogged. Every corner he turned unveiled something new—an alley alive with vibrant murals, the distant toll of a bell tower echoing faintly, or the soft whine of life as antiquity and modernism intertwined seamlessly.

The rhythm of his footsteps melded with the rush of wind, the murmur of voices, and the occasional clang of laughter spilling from open windows. Together, they formed a symphony of city life unfolding around him. The streets ahead seemed to stretch infinitely, beckoning him forward. Each mile told a story, each step an offering to the unyielding pulse of the city— a place that never truly stopped moving.

He eventually slowed and came to a halt; his eyes fixed on the iconic City Hall as if it was the landmark that pulled him in close. It rose like a stone lookout at the heart of the city, a grand testament to history and artistry. Its stature soared skyward, crowned by the imposing sculpture of the city's founder, standing vigilant over the bustling streets below.

The building was a masterpiece of classical and French Renaissance architecture, its faces adorned with sculpted figures, intricate columns, and ornate carvings. Time had toughened the grey limestone, yet it still basked in the sunlight, alive with details of allegorical figures that narrated tales of civic pride and ambition. The clocks stood as silent witnesses to the city's ever-changing pulse, while the soaring tower, with its steeply pitched roofs and elegant curves, echoed an era of timeless elegance.

Crossing Broad Street, he paused briefly, slightly winded but quickly recovering. The fatigue melted away as he pressed forward, headphones playing the final verses of Led Zeppelin's *Stairway to Heaven*. Lost in thought, his heart and lungs felt fully heated, propelling him onward.

He had barely taken a few steps into the street when he noticed the crowd— a dense mob gathered, all fixed on something in the sky to the south. Their heads tilted upward, their collective gaze transfixed. He attempted to bypass them, uninterested in their curiosity. As he moved into the middle of the wide road, an inexplicable sensation stirred deep in his gut—a feeling of unease that made his stomach churn.

His eyes began to itch intensely. He looked up. A human shape hung there, wings working slow and steady. Silence pressed down. One scream cracked it—and the world went dark.

Chapter Two

A Handful of Cheap Flowers

Bars of sunlight striped the sunset across the wall, the room a cell of gold and rust. His stomach complained. Questions circled until they lost their edges, and the room dimmed. He let the dark take him, uneasy, not ready to wake.

The morning sun rose, casting its light through smudged windowpanes that blurred memories of a past life. He cleared his throat and checked his watch—10:42. Lucia's office hours ended at noon. The thought ignited a spark; he yanked on his jacket and bolted.

—Two months earlier—

He was heavier, a full beard roughening his jaw, breath short as he pushed through the fraternity's iron gate—carrying a jolt of inspiration he didn't yet trust. Dark circles etched under his eyes revealed fatigue.

Faded jeans that fit like a memory. A soft, worn leather jacket, mapped with old creases. Boots that had seen things but didn't boast.

After walking a block, he encountered friends, including Matthew, who greeted him with a teasing grin.

"Where you headed looking like you slept under a bridge?" Matthew asked, smirking as he tugged at the collar of his colleague's jacket.

"I'm gonna win her back," he said with determination, laughing lightly at the ribbing.

"Who? Whoa, whoa. You're going to get who back?" Matthew asked, surprised but already knowing the answer.

Matthew separated himself from the group and followed him a few steps. "Her? You mean Lucia?"

"Yeah, of course."

"What? Seriously? What's going on?" Matthew raised an eyebrow.

"Trust me, I know what I'm doing. This is my last chance."

"Dude, I get it, but have you considered that maybe it's over? There are signs, you know?"

"I can't give up without trying. I've got to do this," he said firmly, his heart racing.

He quickened his pace, leaving Matthew shrinking behind him, hearing muffled wishes of good luck in the distance. He crossed the Spring Garden Bridge, the Philadelphia skyline to his right and the Art Museum to his left.

He noted the museum standing like a temple atop its hill, a grand ode to human creativity and resilience. Its neoclassical face, a blend of tawny minerals and seasoned grandeur, glowed in the shifting daylight. Corinthian columns stood in stately sequence, guarding the treasures within, while intricate murals alleged tales of myth and ambition.

A staircase of heroic proportions poured down before it, a path to triumph for the bold who run or climb its steps, their taunts and conquests reverberating through the air. At its summit, the museum's bronze doors glinted defiantly against the elements, a gateway to imagined worlds—preserved history. Behind it, the Schuylkill River wound like a silver ribbon.

As he hurried, he reflected on the city's historic nature, established centuries before he was born, how it would endure long after he was dead and buried. *We were only renting this space.*

Moving up the Benjamin Franklin Parkway toward the train station, he entered the bustling transportation center, marveling at its massive ceilings and intricate design. 30th Street opened like a cathedral—light gushing through tall windows, chandeliers floating over the marble hush. He slowed without meaning to. The ceiling's Art Deco geometry held his gaze.

Wooden benches, worn smooth by decades of waiting, offered a place for pause beneath the station's regal embrace. A great bronze statue welcomed people entering from the East doors, an angel with wings fully upright in eternal ascent, holding an individual—symbolizing the freeing of youth from the flames of battle. He soon remembered why he'd come and kept moving—flowers, not worship.

Amid the hustle and bustle, he was acutely aware of his thoughts, contemplating whether resolving his negative feelings was even possible by getting her back.

In the distance, the flower vendor's booth drew him in with the prospect of affordable bouquets. Spotting the stand tucked away in the corner, the keeper never looked idle—snipping away extraneous stems and dying petals, all the while serving a steady stream of customers who hurriedly grabbed his products for their loved ones.

As he approached the booth, a sudden halt interrupted his steps. To his right, a solo guitarist warmed up with random notes. The acoustic melody of *Just Like Heaven* filled the air with the haphazard strums of the novice. The coincidence of the song choice prompted a common yet unspoken thought. *Is the universe fucking with me? Is there some god-like creature, bored in the heavens, making fun of me for his sick amusement?*

Despite his fleeting skepticism, he proceeded to the flower shop owner, fumbling to gather a meager sum from his pocket. Gazing at the assortment of flowers, he decided that red roses were the most fitting.

"This enough for a few roses?" he asked, extending his palm of crumpled bills and coins.

The man weighed the money with a glance, already reaching. "Baby's Breath today," he said, swift and polite, and passed him a small cluster.

Fitting, he thought bitterly; all he could afford was a filler flower meant to accompany something grander. As he gazed at the delicate, star-like blossoms clustered together, they seemed ethereal—a frothy veil of simplicity.

Exiting the station, he noticed dark clouds gathering. A low rumble of thunder signaled the approaching rain. Determined to shield the flowers from the downpour, he hurried back toward campus, the air growing heavier with each step.

As dusk fell and the rain began to pour, he turned onto her street. There she was—Lucia—descending the steps of her apartment, her umbrella shielding her from the storm. A smile tugged at the corners of his lips despite his pounding heart.

"Lucia!" he called.

And then he knew—this wasn't now. This was a memory replaying, somewhere beyond the living. Rain stitched the street and bit at him.

She paused, her steps faltering as she heard his voice. Slowly, she turned her back to him, standing under her teal umbrella while he remained exposed in the heavy shower.

There it is. He tilted his face upward, raindrops splattering against his skin, and spotted the radiant, impossibly white moon in the sky, its famous feline grin glowing mischievously.

With the flowers in his hand hanging low, he slowly absorbed the moment before raising his eyes again.

"This was the last time I ever saw you," he murmured, his expression teetering between a smile and a frown. The warmth of the memory enveloped him. She remained with her back turned, and he raised a hand to his face, rediscovering the sensation of rain after what felt like eons wandering in the dark.

Each droplet descended like a soft footstep, tapping upon leaves and soil with delicate tempo. It was a hushed applause from the heavens, a gentle patter that grew and receded like the breathing of the world. The air hummed with freshness, the scent of damp earth rising to meet the melody. Tiny streams formed, their trickles adding harmony, while the occasional plop of a heavier drop punctuated the soothing cadence. In this gentle serenade, time slowed, and nature's song wrapped itself around their souls.

"Just a few ages, and I guess this is the best so far. The back of your head. That beautiful back of your head," he mused. The street was devoid of other human life. She seemed perpetually on the verge of turning around, breathing heavily, but remained steadfast. She hadn't turned around when this moment first happened an eternity ago; she couldn't turn around now.

Her hair—midnight falling with whispers—tumbled in endless spirals, as though each curl danced with secrets confided only by the stars. It moved like a living river, wild yet gentle, every strand a story, every wave a memory. He recalled how it once framed her face; a crown of unruly elegance that shadowed her eyes just enough to make him ache to see them more clearly.

He longed to reach out, to touch it—soft as the first light of dawn, fragrant like summer's deepest bloom. The way her hair caught the wind, teasing and untamed, mirrored a freedom he could never cage, nor would he want to. In her absence, he felt the void it left behind—a black ocean that once flowed through his fingers but was now forever beyond his reach.

"It was only three words, and I blew it. You meant so much to me, and I thought... expressing my feelings meant stepping into a whole new chapter of my life," he reflected.

Uncertain if his words were for her or merely an awakening for himself, he continued. "It doesn't matter now, I know. I'm still trying to find you; I won't give up. I feel like I'm getting close; I just hope you're okay. I'm so alone, and I see nothing but darkness."

The sound of his breath rose and fell, a hymn trembling with longing, echoing softly in the peaceful world. Each exhale carried a confession, unspoken but deeply felt, while each inhale drew in a fragile promise of hope. His breathing was a lullaby and a storm—a pattern of vulnerability, a soul laid bare. It resonated in the stillness, a melody only the rain seemed to hear.

The silver crescent moon floated in the velvet night with a condescending smirk, its delicate curve glowing with faint luminescence. It hung low on the horizon, like a pearl cradled in shadow. Wisps of translucent cloud caressed its edges, softening its light into a dreamlike shimmer. Its grin was knowing—a secret shared with the rest of the sky, as if it held the laughter of the tides it seemed to control. The reflection of its light on the still puddles below doubled its joy, dancing with the rhythm of the earth's stillness.

A raindrop clung to the tip of his black boot like a tiny jewel poised to fall. Feeling a sudden pang of distress, he lowered his head to stare at it. The gloomy clouds rolled across the sky, and the moon withdrew. Slowly, darkness gathered once more, the bitter cold returning, swallowing everything around him—until, perhaps, another hopeful glimpse emerged.

Chapter Three

A Battle on Broad Street

Blackness thinned. He snapped his headphones off; sound rushed in—sirens, heat, the sting of ash in his throat. People's phones lifted, necks craned to the sky. Above them, something hovered—an angelic shape devoid of peace.

Car alarms wailed, thick smoke curled into the air, and flames flickered like vengeful spirits. The streets were alive with shouts, a cacophony of fear and confusion as people recorded the surreal moment.

Suspicion and paranoia jumped from person to person. Shoulders slammed. A stroller wheel spun where nobody stood. In the distance, an overturned truck belched fumes beneath the winged figure, which began to descend, vanishing from view behind the crowd. The gravity of the situation struck him—everything was unraveling, the city collapsing into chaos.

He wondered, in a fleeting moment of clarity, Is this the last day of my life?

A car hurtled through the air, its metallic scream piercing the chaos. It crashed to the ground nearby, crushing a group of onlookers in its path. Bodies scattered like leaves in the wind, everyone running in every direction, desperate to escape. While the crowd surged around him, thumping into him in their panic, he stood firm—unmovable, like a fixed object in the face of an unstoppable force.

The street was a grim tableau of slag and cinders, everything coated in ruin. Another fleeing figure collided with him, falling backward upon impact—hurt. Their expressions twisted in horror as they looked up at him, their fear deepening as they scrambled away.

Something pressed behind his eyes, a cold, widening pressure he didn't understand. A strange calm overtook him, warring with the fear that clawed at his mind. Instead of escaping, he felt compelled to move toward the danger. The screams and noise faded into an eerie silence; only the wind in the skeletal trees remained.

The sunlight above was bright, yet shadows pooled unnaturally across the ground. Without conscious thought, he began to run toward the figure, determination etched into every step.

Through the dust and wreckage, he sprinted, dodging flying debris and navigating the devastation with an agility that surprised him. A hand clamped his throat. The street yawned, and then he was airborne—an arc, a blur, the blind flash of glass. He hit the masonry hard enough to spider the pane. His ears rang; breath tore from him. It should have hurt. His body understood the blow even if the pain didn't land.

A deep, primal rage simmered. He gazed upward, only to be seized by the neck once again, pinned against the building's wall, feet dangling above the ground. The assailant was him—this creature wore his face, with full black eyes that swallowed the light, and bright white angelic wings spanning twenty feet on either side.

It was an ethereal paradox cloaked in radiant menace. Wings unfurled—too clean for what stared back. The eyes held no mercy, no life, only the cold promise of despair. It paced with reverence. Every step carried the weight of wars, every beat of its wings echoed with the anguished cries of a corrupted grace. It was a flame that burned cold, a light that blinded with the darkness it hid.

Dressed identically to him, the mirror image peered into his eyes without uttering a word. It released him, and he descended to the ground, bewildered and shaken. Coughing, panting, and teary-eyed in sheer terror, he slumped against the building, seated on the ground, overwhelmed by horror and anxiety. The angel, with its back now turned, disregarded him.

The surrounding crowd retreated to a safer distance while still witnessing in disbelief—phones in hand. The being extended its right hand to the side, summoning a sword-like weapon into its grasp, as if from a dense black tear in space.

Still breathing frantically on the ground, a second sword materialized in front of him, dropping from a temporary blackish narrow hole six feet off the ground. It clanged vividly as it bounced on the asphalt once and then lay there.

The sword stood as a relic, a monumental testament to the artistry of a place unknown. Its blade, impossibly large yet unnervingly graceful, was forged from iridescent metal that shifted in hue from every angle—deep indigo at its core, streaked with veins of molten gold that rippled like living veins. Along its surface, faint, indiscernible inscriptions danced and shimmered.

The hilt was wrapped in leather that seemed aged yet unyielding, its texture alive with the impressions of hands that once gripped it with unshakable resolve. A faint aura surrounded the weapon, a soft yet menacing glow that whispered of its otherworldly origins.

His eyes widened at the sight, and in a desperate attempt to distance himself from the unfolding surrealism, he kicked the sword away, screaming, "What do you want?! Please! What is this? Help! Somebody help!" He yelled, but no one came near.

Frustration mounted within the creature; it became furious, prompting it to cast aside its own sword. Swiftly turning around, it executed a forceful kick, slamming his head into the building. As pain registered, he gauged the intensity, likening it to being playfully struck. He felt no tangible discomfort, rising to a standing position with hands raised, pleading once more, "Please, whatever you want—just tell me what you want!"

Abruptly dragged to the middle of the street, he experienced a powerful throw that propelled him upward through the smoke, soaring then crashing through the windows of a towering high-rise. Landing in an under-construction area within the building's office floor, he lay immobile, trying to process the moment—again unharmed.

In a continued state of panic, muttering to himself amid the discord of screams and sirens fading from the streets below, he desperately scanned his surroundings for help. Making his way toward the fire staircase door, he grabbed the handle only to have it ripped off effortlessly. Pausing for a moment, he decided to test the developing theory. With a slight knock from his fist, the fire door became unhinged, clattering down the steps. Disturbing screams echoed from above, prompting him to rush upward instead of descending.

Entering the office space, he found people gazing out the window, their eyes widening with terror as they spotted him. They were whispering something. Catching a reflection of himself in an internal window, he noticed his eyes were entirely black in dilation, matching that of the adversary below.

Urgently, he implored, "Please, everybody, we need to get out of here." He channeled his memories of heroes in popular movies, with an internal motivation forming to guide others to safety before himself. Jarring thoughts flooded his mind in an instant. If he lived long enough, the world might all be lost for him to witness as a voyeur. The burden of all perishing and being left as a sole survivor.

A series of rumbles from the base of the building gagged everyone on the floor into deathly silence. Like the tremors of an earthquake, the building vibrated and shook, the sound of steel whining and breaking. Soon, the sound of shattering glass and people wailing filled the air. The building began screeching and started to lean to one side, visible through the windows along one wall. The floor became slanted, and demented panic ensued. Some rushed down the fire staircase, while others huddled under desks or curled up in the fetal position.

Cubicles, desks, and appliances toppled as people and objects slid toward the wall of cascading windows. The building groaned, inching toward a collision with the one next to it, just fifty feet away. He knew to punch through the carpet, grab onto the subfloor, and hold on, tendons burning, boots skidding until the slide stopped. People crashed into the glass panes as the building slammed into the adjacent structure. Fright took over as a large copy machine flew from the other side of the room and shattered the wall of windows, sending several people plummeting outward.

Quick on his feet, he grabbed two people, unintentionally tossing them inward due to his uncontrolled strength. He then fell diagonally toward the windows as their world tilted. Turning around and pressing his face against the glass, he was forced to look in horror as people fell from the floors above and below him.

The sky felt heavier than ever, painted in muted grays as chaos unfolded below. The sharp crackle of flames and the wailing sirens drowned out every thought. Time splintered. He wanted to shout, to beg them to hold on, but the screams around him rose to a crescendo.

Their arms outstretched as if reaching for impossible salvation while they fell. The sound of their descent was swallowed by the roar of the inferno and the gasps of the crowd. But the impact—each one—was unmistakable, an awful punctuation to a moment no one could stop.

The scene blurred through his tears, those images burned into memory: faces contorted with terror, hands clawing for safety, and the unrelenting pull of gravity. Any hope of saving those around him was crushed by the scale of the massacre and the devastating realization that he could not save every soul.

Struggling to regain his composure, he crawled back to the center of the building floor, where a silhouette appeared at the far end of the office space. The figure outside the opposite wall of windows made it painfully apparent.

He should've taken the blade. That had been the rule, whatever it was—and this was the cost of breaking it.

As the building leveled off against the one it had crashed into, his expression shifted from fear to anger. He sprinted toward the figure, climbing diagonally and crashing through the windows. He grabbed the angel mid-air. The creature ascended, and he gripped its neck, trying to strangle it as it picked up speed. Then it abruptly dove downward, hurtling both headfirst toward a large traffic circle with a fountain at its center.

The impact slammed him into the sidewalk, the being unscathed, forming a crater that exposed reinforcing steel and crumbled concrete beneath the plaza. The force was akin to being hit by a speeding car, leaving him struggling to recover. He could not get up.

Water shot up from the fountain while sunlight filtered through it, casting an array of colors onto the oily liquid, the sound pattering down on the surface. No civilians were in sight; he felt cold and alone. The soothing sound of the water was challenged by the figure's wings casting a vast shadow over him. He lay on the pavement, facing the ground as it approached.

He was grabbed by the arm and forced into a kneeling position, reminiscent of an execution. The angel taunted him with the sword, standing behind him and pressing the cold steel against the back of his neck before steadily raising it to the sky.

Tires screamed. Doors slammed, radios crackled—"Hold your fire—Clear the line!"

"Open fire!"

The rounds stitched the air; white feathers tore loose after the command from a police chief blurted out in the distance. A swarm of officers and military personnel unleashed gunfire onto the being. It flinched but didn't fall.

In a burst of movement, he noticed the shadow of the figure had shifted. He lifted himself amidst the ongoing gunfire. Mouth agape and panting in exhaustion, he planted his right elbow into the concrete, then quickly bent his legs toward his abdomen and released a double kick into the angel's legs, slamming them into the fountain's cement base. The sword dropped from its hand. Catching it mid-air after a single bounce, he sliced through the angel's neck from left to right; the top half of its torso slid off. Pure dark liquid spewed in every direction from the adversary, mixing with the fountain water and generating a pool of dense blackness around them.

Hazel bled back into his eyes. He doubled over and retched, tasting metal. Everything smelled of dampness and rot. Seen through blurriness, he was surrounded by those in uniform with vehicles and guns still drawn. The sound of a helicopter whirred overhead; he was drowning in the struggle to stay awake.

Losing consciousness, his vision fading, his cheek slammed onto the exposed aggregate surface. The liquid from his mouth mixed with that of the roaring fountain. His eyes closed.

Chapter Four

A Little Too Much to Drink

It was a temperate night. Loud, deafening music pulsed throughout the club. The deep bass reverberated from a giant black speaker on the stage, vibrating the air around him. At this time, he was significantly overweight, with a disheveled goatee. His hair, wiry and unkempt, was brushed haphazardly back.

The atmosphere hummed, thick with the scent of desire and electric rebellion. Beams of light fractured and flickered, dancing like restless spirits across a sea of bodies, each one moving to the beats.

The walls thudded, draped in inky blackness, swallowing whispers and laughter alike, while the bassline throbbed like a heartbeat—primal and unrelenting. In corners shrouded in half-light, stories were exchanged in murmurs and glances, their endings lost in the haze of forgotten hours.

A kaleidoscope of muted colors flickered over faces, catching the gleam of sweat and the glint of eyes brimming with secret hunger. Here, time dripped slowly, stretching moments into infinity, where the only truth was the music's relentless sway and the magnetic pull of the shadows alive with possibility.

He clocked a knot of students muscling in beside him, their empty glasses already raised. The bartender—forearm ink—moved fast. With drinks in hand, they made their way onto the dance floor, reminding him of the companionship he no longer possessed. Most of the crowd awaited the upcoming rock band, while others congregated around the long bars for discounted beer specials.

Frustrated by his repeated failures to catch the bartender's attention, his annoyance grew as more people were served before him. Waving his hand, coughing purposefully, and leaning forward—each time, the extremely attractive bartender with the low-cut top and bleach-blonde hair failed to acknowledge him.

Finally, after what felt like an eternity, their eyes met.

"Three lagers?" he asked.

"Coming up," she replied, her voice tinged with annoyance.

He slid coins and a crumpled bill.

She set the bottles down flat. "You know we live on tips, right?"

Heat climbed his neck. "Just trying to make it last longer," he muttered to no one, as she had already walked away.

Shouldering through the thick crowd of dancers, he searched for his fraternity brothers, lost in the ocean of drunken students. He spotted Luke thanks to his imposing stature—standing tall at 6'5" and weighing 220 pounds of solid muscle. His distinctive South Korean features made him easily recognizable in the dimly lit establishment.

He smoothly sidled up beside him, effortlessly balancing two bottles of beer in one hand while extending another bottle to Luke with the other, wordlessly offering it.

"Wait, seriously?" he exclaimed, noticing that Luke already had three bottles of the same beer. "I told you I was grabbing—"

He shrugged and broke into a hearty laugh before he could finish his reprimand.

Luke took one bottle from his hand and capped the other two with napkins to prevent them from foaming. He didn't say much; he never did. Always scanning exits, the stage, the crowd—he saw patterns the rest of them missed. He had formed a bond with him like Matthew, but for different reasons. Luke had been inspired by his leadership when he was president of the fraternity, watching in awe as his friend united a house full of jocks, nerds, borderline drug addicts, and assholes—transforming a house on the brink of collapse into one poised for resurgence. Ever since, Luke had been drawn to close camaraderie.

A thoughtful, inquisitive individual with a strong academic focus, Luke was the type of student who enjoyed deep research, meticulous about details—traits that reflected his future as a physician and historian. A blend of intellectual rigor and a compassionate heart, Luke strove to make a difference on campus and beyond—but he barely ever spoke.

"Now where's Ma—" Before he could finish asking, Matthew suddenly appeared in front of them, holding three identical beers, just like the others.

They shared an amused glance. Without another word, he deftly slipped one bottle into each side pocket of his pants and raised the remaining bottle to his lips, taking a long sip while staring at Matthew and Luke with a furrowed brow.

Amid the cheerful chatter and laughter, Matthew's expression turned serious as he gestured toward the women seated at the bar. "Check out those girls," he nudged, nearly shouting to be heard over the noise.

"What about them?" he replied without looking up.

"They were just looking over here, I think?" Matthew said, his voice filled with intrigue.

He barely glanced over, showing no interest in any attempts to lighten the mood.

"Stop thinking about her," Matthew urged, leaning in as his voice fought against the bass. "You're surrounded. Pick anyone." He pointed toward the dance floor. "There. The girl with the black hair."

As he considered approaching the young woman on the dance floor, he noticed, *it was her.*

Lucia moved as if she owned the song. Black locks spilled and caught the light. Her eyes held a quiet intensity that drew him in. Strength and grace coexisted in the lines of her hips, shoulders, and the clean turn of her wrist. The dress shimmered when she laughed. His heart raced like he'd been running.

"Shit," Matthew muttered, his eyes widening as he recognized the figure in the distance.

He stood transfixed, staring intently at her. Everything else around him seemed to vanish. In that moment, there was no one else—just the two of them and a thumping bass.

"Dude, let's... we can just leave. Let's go to another bar," Matthew suggested, catching up to him and placing a hand on his shoulder.

He remained silent, his gaze locked on Lucia. A strong desire to speak with her bubbled up within him. Matthew shook his head, knowing his efforts were futile.

He quickly finished his beer, tossing the empty bottle into a nearby trash can. "Again," Matthew muttered to Luke, who stood beside him.

Lucia was a vision of grace and fire. Her long shadowy curls cascaded like a waterfall, voiceless, with riddles of untold beauty. Her deep, soulful brown eyes glowed with a quiet intensity, like sunlit earth after rain, drawing him in with their tender depth.

Her physique, sculpted and agile, spoke of strength and softness in perfect harmony. The curve of her hips and the arch of her back danced with sensuality and confidence, leaving him breathless. The world itself seemed to bend to her will.

Without a word, he made his way toward Lucia, leaving his fraternity brothers fading into the background. He stopped at arm's length, palms open. "Can we talk?" he asked, his voice low and tight. "Please—just over here."

Something flickered in her face—half a beat off from the music. The room felt a fraction delayed. "I'm sorry," she said too calmly, and he knew he was back inside a memory.

Now aware of the illusion trapping them, he simply responded, "I know."

The bond between them had once felt profound, but now it was frayed in many ways. Time seemed to freeze as they stood facing each other, the world around them fading away. It was just the two of them, alone in that moment. The temperature was blazing.

Feeling calm, he looked at Lucia's right leg. Despite her short skirt, her scar was nearly invisible now. In that moment of stillness, she softly said, "I never said thank you for that."

Suddenly, a guy bore between them, reaching for Lucia. The shove caught him off balance; the punch landed before he could blink. Floor. Lights. Noise. He lay sprawled on the ground.

The bottles cracked in his pockets and spilled cold across his legs. Stale beer and perfume burned his nose. Laughter echoed above him as he tried to rise and slid again.

The initial impact was sharp and disorienting, his body slamming against a tacky, grimy surface that felt like a mixture of spilled drinks, sweat, and grease. The floor was littered with wet patches, smashed cocktail glasses, half-eaten food, and traces of cigarette butts.

The sensation of being suddenly surrounded by that filth made his skin crawl. He felt the cool, damp stickiness of spilled liquor clinging to his clothes and skin, while the lingering smells filled his nostrils. His hands pressed against the gluey floor, and he felt immediate revulsion, as if the dirtiness was leeching into his body. Each attempt to rise reminded him of the countless people who had walked over that very spot—some dragging in mud, some spilling drinks, and some leaving traces of bodily fluids. The sounds of dancing, chatting, and laughter around him contrasted sharply with the sinking feeling of isolation as he lay there, feeling both exposed and mortified.

The man held him firmly in his gaze, bent down, and stretched his back. He turned his neck from left to right, popping it with a series of rapid clicks. The crowd roared with laughter as he struggled to get up, more beer spraying out, making him even more embarrassed. Reliving this memory, floating endlessly through time and space, felt like an unnecessary cruelty.

The bouncers arrived quickly, mistaking him for the intoxicated aggressor. He found himself on the sidewalk before the first chord from the stage finished, stumbling into a stack of trash bags. One split under his cheek with a sour puff of air. Inside, the music thumped on without him.

The muffled sound of music behind the closed doors of the club sent a chill up his spine; the statistical probability that the song playing would be this one seemed unfathomable. Through the building's external wall, the suppressed lyrics mixed with the commotion of partygoers.

From inside, a cover band paying tribute to The Cure leaked through the wall—*Just Like Heaven*. Two words—*show me*—made his stomach drop. He was haunted by a song created in a simpler time, one that evoked intense emotions associated with romantic love. The lyrics expressed the feeling of being both overwhelmed and exhilarated by passion, drawing from the sensation of being lifted or transported to a euphoric state. The imagery of two lovers in a dreamlike state conveyed a longing to relive those moments of joy and wonder once more.

Melancholy and stench, paired with crushing pain, washed over him. There was no one around. For his own therapeutic needs, he looked up directly into the sky, knowing what he would see. The brisk air made his breath rise upward. That same Cheshire cat smile, laughing at his expense from a million miles away. The thin moon hung there like a cut fingernail, pale and mean. It represented a universe amused. He felt cold and weightless. His mind fell away into intimate darkness.

Chapter Five

A Party of the '80s Variety

The ambulance siren faded in and out as he regained consciousness, strapped to a stretcher with his face hidden under an oxygen mask, struggling to blink against the harsh fluorescent lights overhead. Overcome with anxiety, he fought to remember how he ended up there. His thoughts were jumbled, but one thing was certain: he had to locate Lucia. *Where are you?*

"Eyes open. Good!" one of the paramedics shouted.

"Restraints—tighten."

"Needle in."

"Hold him down!"

He whirled in fear when he saw the syringe. His foot came loose from his explosive thrashing, giving him the chance to kick the needle out of the paramedic's hand. It clanked to the ground, and the paramedics let out a shocked cry. Seizing the opportunity, he pushed the gurney closer to the ambulance's back door, using his weight to lift himself repeatedly from the bed against the straps.

One of the paramedics yelled, "Stop him!" but it was too late.

Using the metallic bars of the mobile hospital bed, he jostled his entire body vertically, and as he came down, his foot caught the red lever. The doors flew open. Tires squealing and horns honking, he and the gurney slammed onto the wet road. Rain poured down, hazy yellow headlights in every direction, and cars swerved to avoid him. The metal rails on the bed broke upon impact as it scraped to a halt. He lurched to his feet and bolted, sprinting faster than he ever felt possible, escaping the chaotic scene as the ambulance screeched to a stop. Police vehicles that had been following turned to pursue him.

The sun had set. Bleeding and gasping for air, he paused after countless blocks in an unknown direction, panting and leaning against a building. Attracted by the commotion, a group of individuals approached with arrogant grins and sarcastic laughs. A bottle broke.

"Where'd you escape from, bro?" one of them said.

"Empty your pockets," another demanded.

"Please," he begged, barely catching his breath. "I don't want any trouble— I just need to find... someone."

"Yeah, right," a broad-shouldered man taunted, shoving him against the wall.

Desperation turned to anger. "I'm serious. Just leave me alone."

He swung at the burly accoster, but the punch went wide.

The man's chuckle echoed through the deserted, puddle-strewn street. The others joined in, surrounding him.

"What was that?" one hissed, punching him in the gut. The air was knocked out of him, and he doubled over. A barrage of punches and kicks followed, leaving him with no time to react. All he could comprehend was the wrenching pain. Each blow felt worse than the last. *Where'd the strength go that I had only an hour ago?*

He caught a flash of metal at his waistband. On the next swing, he trapped the man's wrist to his hip, pivoted, and tore the gun free. "Back off!" His voice shook but held firm.

Their eyes widened in astonishment at the sight of the weapon, causing them to raise their hands and scatter. An image of dread and desperation was reflected in their flight. The assailants' footsteps echoed against brick walls as their shadows melted into the night's obscurity.

His hands trembled as he grasped the weapon. The cool metal felt foreign, heavier than he had expected. His fingers curled around it, tracing its contours like an unspoken truth. Its smooth surface contradicted the storm brewing in his mind.

The steel was slick, like the sharp quiet before a clap of thunder. He felt the heartbeat of his palm against the gun. A strange mix of power and fragility coiled in his chest, echoing the emotions he had felt earlier. This small yet immense object could shatter or still with a single touch. The heaviness was not just physical but a weight of choice, of inevitability. He flexed his grip, testing it. In a sudden flash of recognition, the gun felt like a silent partner.

Police sirens grew louder. The flashing red and blue lights were approaching. He hastily tucked the revolver into the back of his pants and dashed toward a stand of trees.

A police car's searchlight sliced through the darkness, covering the alley where he had stood moments before. His pulse thumped in his chest as he leaned against the coarse bark of an oak tree and watched the light pass by.

He took a deep breath under the cool, protective shade of the foliage. The world felt heavy, the blackness enveloping him like a burdensome blanket. In despair, he mumbled incoherently to himself. *Why is this happening?* His teeth ground; breath sawed through the scent of a mask still lingering in his nose. Thoughts raced, trying to make sense of the disarray that had overtaken his life so abruptly. Occasionally, a vehicle horn or a yell would pierce through the distant buzz of the metropolis. It all felt like an unreal backdrop to an increasingly severe nightmare.

He walked and glanced up at the street signs in the city he had lived in his whole life—lost, searching for any clue that might lead him. His mumbling erupted into a rhetorical scream, confident that the police were blocks away. "Where am I?!"

As if the city heard him, he noticed the muffled, unearthly symphony of distinct 90s rock blended with electronic dance music drifting through the buildings from miles away. Two huge purple beams of light suddenly shot high into the sky, swaying back and forth, accompanying the playlist and leading a direct path to a party that had apparently just begun. He muttered to himself for his own amusement again, "That's not 80s music, Mark," and started to run toward the timely beacon. The bass thumped off glass and brick, guiding him like a compass.

He pushed past the agony, even though his legs felt heavy and his muscles protested with every stride. His concentrated mind barely registered the swirl of hues as the neon lights of the city flashed past him. As he navigated the streets, the noise of the city faded to a muffled din in his ears. It was pure focus, pure purpose.

The music grew louder as he neared the fraternity house, lightning and thunder taking turns echoing in the sky, merging with the pounding bass in his bones. Rain began to fall hard. The intensity of the purple lights increased, casting an unsettling, mesmerizing glow over the area. Every deep thud of the music resonated with the beating of his heart, and he could feel the pulsating tunes.

Ahead, the fraternity's black front door stood slightly ajar, letting light and music spill into the night. The spectacle within hit him as soon as he burst through the entrance. People danced wildly, drinks spilled everywhere, and laughter bounced off the chaotic house's walls—everyone dressed in 1980s attire. The stench of sweat and alcohol permeated the air, and the flashing lights created an unsettling strobe effect. Pushing through the crowd, he scanned the room for someone he recognized.

Despite the flashing lights and smoke, he spotted a familiar face. "Mark!" he yelled above the din, his voice barely audible. His heart raced as he pushed past people, each second stretching out before him.

Mark clocked him. "What's with your eyes?" he asked in that calm podcast voice, already palming his phone and assuming his mentor was in some sort of costume.

Mark's relationship with him was strong, but different from most. Their friendship, based on similarities, had been shaped by the "big brother" and "little brother" structure of the fraternity, even though they were only six months apart in age.

A journalism major, Mark was heavily involved in campus media, writing for the school newspaper and creating videos about human connection and spiritual journeys. With a curious mind and a sharp eye for detail, Mark often shared stories that resonated with his peers, focusing on core truths.

A shorter man with bronzed skin and light eyes, he preferred simple, comfortable clothes, like hoodies and jeans. Mark was slightly introverted, but, like many in the fraternity, alcohol and drugs brought out personalities that masked their true selves.

"No time to explain," he replied urgently. "I need you to gather all the pledges. Now."

Mark hesitated, glancing at the revelers. "Dude, everyone's pretty wasted already."

"I don't care," he snapped, grabbing Mark by the shoulder. "It's important. Get them together and get everyone out of the basement."

Mark nodded, sensing the gravity of the situation. "Alright, I'll get them. But—" He was cut off as his phone was snatched from his hand.

"You have Lucia's number in here, right?"

Mark nodded, then disappeared into the crowd. He quickly fumbled with the device's settings to ensure it remained unlocked. Scanning the room, his eyes landed on it. Another angelic version of himself stood by the back door, smirking and staring back at him. Ignoring the fear gnawing at him, he carefully pulled the gun from his waistband and fumbled to hold it firmly. He saw Mark emerge from the basement steps and give a thumbs up. Without hesitation, he pointed the gun, cringed, and fired three deafening shots into the hardwood floor beside him.

Three concussions cracked the song in half. Smoke and splinters lifted from the floor; ears rang. The room froze—then broke. "What the hell, man?" someone yelled as bodies shoved for the door.

"Get out!" he roared, waving the revolver. "Everyone, out of the house!"

Something slammed into his head—images, not words. Clarity consumed him all at once and triggered enormous pain. He dropped the gun as it was kicked out the front door by fleeing shoes. *They want a fight*, he realized. *Before the extermination, they chose me because I didn't run.*

Determined, he walked toward the second angel, its wings spreading wide as the crowd screamed and ran. The battle commenced fiercely, with punches and throws demolishing the fraternity house. They crashed through walls, immediately ascending from the second to the third floor, leaving destruction in their wake.

His resolve was fueled by the burning desire to find Lucia. He used all his strength to battle the impenetrable body, pounding it with his hands and feet. If he were to survive this, there was still time to find her before the end of everything. The angel struck with equal ferocity, its otherworldly might evident in every blow. The surroundings seemed to quake, as though even the buildings were terrified of the apocalyptic conflict.

The battle tore through rooms, smashing furniture and hurling debris in every direction. The air was filled with broken glass, twisted metal, and splintered wood—a chaotic maelstrom of devastation. They fought on, their struggle echoing through the night, with grunts of exertion, the cracking of bones, and the crumbling of stone creating a violent symphony.

Rain poured through the roof's new openings as they battled, each drop a chilling, painful reminder of the world beyond their fight. Both were drenched, the slick ground beneath them making every move more treacherous. Rainwater mixed with sweat and blood, forming scarlet streams that ran down their bodies. Every blow felt like it was tearing him apart, his nerves buzzing with agony. Yet, he pressed on, driven by her memory and his need to keep her safe.

Eventually, the angel seized him by the shoulder and, with effortless strength, lifted him off the ground. A jolt of power rattled his bones, and he gasped as his vision blurred. He was hurled onto the bed, crashing against it before tumbling across the floor.

His cat, Jersey, meowed pitifully from under the crushed bed, her eyes wide with terror, reflecting his own. The battle had spilled into his room.

Seeing Jersey sparked a renewed surge of energy. He winked at her. "It's gonna be okay, sweetie," he whispered. He stood up grinning.

Ignoring the pain, he lunged at the angel, tackling it with a primal roar. They plowed through the front brick wall of the mansion, the impact sending shards and chunks of blocks flying. They landed heavily in the yard, sinking into the soaked grass and mud beneath them.

The angel on top pressed his head deep into the sludge. He couldn't breathe, submerged, and with one eye open to the right, he saw why the figure only had one hand in use. The other gripped the familiar sword, which had once again appeared from the ether. His right hand grasped the creature's sword hand while his face sank deeper into the black mud, his vision obscured. His left hand flailed desperately, searching. It swept through mud and glass—steel. The gun. As the angel lifted the sword with both hands, preparing to deliver a fatal blow, he tore it free from the muck and fired into the thing's throat.

With desperation clawing at him, he made one final attempt, mirroring his previous actions. He grasped the back of the angel's neck and hurled its body several feet toward the centuries-old black iron fence, its neck landing on the spikes. He pulled down with all his weight, the creature's weakened throat pressing against the sharp, timeless metal. He screamed, his voice echoing down the street, using every ounce of strength to pull downward. With a sickening snap, the angel's head broke free from its body, black blood scattered in gruesome arcs.

The once luminous being now stood as a hollow wreck of false divinity, bathed in the pale glow of a disappearing moon. Its alabaster wings, once proud, trembled, their faint rustling mourning their own existence. The body thrashed violently, arms flailing through the air in desperate, silent screams—a grotesque dance of death. It staggered, wings beating once, twice, then folding like wet canvas. Black spray threaded through the rain.

With no head to guide it and no mind to think, the body stumbled forward, its wings crumpling under the weight of its misery. It collapsed to the earth with an unholy thud, its fractured limbs twitching in futile spasms. The soaked ground drank blood as the last vestiges of its light flickered and crashed.

Exhausted, he tossed the severed skull aside, barely able to breathe. He slumped beside it, a dark and foul taste rising in his mouth. He spat it out, his vision swimming. Around him, the frightened screams of spectators faded into the distance, a haunting chorus. He could barely make out their faces, twisted in horror and awe—a sea of illuminated cell phones. He gathered the last of his strength to utter a single word, the name that had driven him through this nightmare.

"Lucia," he said, his voice barely a whisper. The void took him again.

Chapter Six

A Babysitting Gig

The sound of the doorbell ricocheted through the muted night, a sharp, unexpected sound against the stillness. The door was a slab of obsidian, closed, concealing the visitor from view. It stood solemnly, commanding its frame. It absorbed the lamp's brilliance, transforming it into a painting of mysteries, where faint reflections of the world flitted and faded.

The door's edges were sharp as a dark horizon, outlined in fine silver where dusk yielded—a frame of modest authority, a gateway unknown, neither inviting nor forbidding, simply waiting. The handle gleamed like an unspoken promise, a polished curve of cold steel resting in anticipation of the hand that dared to twist it.

She opened the entry and blinked, breath catching. He saw her take a small half-step back before she found a smile.

"Hey," he murmured, his voice teasingly tense. He had an ungainly build beneath his jacket, and his stubbled beard gave him a rough appearance that contrasted with the clean-shaven man she'd known. A growing beer belly protruded from beneath his shirt, more noticeable than ever, a reflection of the strain and late hours he'd spent wallowing.

"Hey." Lucia glanced past him, then back. "Why are you here?" Despite her struggle with melancholy, her eyes remained warm. No smile reached her lips. She hesitated before moving forward and giving him a tepid embrace, a gesture suggesting their shared history with fleeting emotions.

He held her, the scent of the forest after rain rushing back to him—familiar as a dog-eared page. For a moment, he forgot to breathe. The faint sweetness of wild jasmine lingered like her laughter in the silence when they were at their best.

As he leaned closer, he caught a whisper of vanilla, soft and inviting, blending with the fresh, clean notes of morning droplets kissed by sunlight. It was a fragrance that wrapped around his senses, grounding him while leaving him adrift. Her hair smelled like the pages of a book he never finished, each strand telling a story of intimacy—both acquainted and intoxicating—drawing him closer, as if her very essence had been woven into the curls.

"I thought... maybe you'd want company," he said, looking into her eyes.

Her smile didn't reach her eyes. "Come in."

As he entered, his eyes adjusted to the dim hallway light. The house was silent, the kind of silence that results from children being asleep. He noticed a few tiny shoes near the door and toys scattered across the living room floor. His gaze landed on Lucia's right leg, still bearing the scar from months prior. She hobbled slightly.

"So, you're babysitting tonight?" he asked, glancing around the room. "It's like an oven in here, by the way."

Lucia nodded, a tender expression on her face. "Yeah, I'm just watching over my neighbor's kids. They're good kids—just a handful."

Just then, little footsteps echoed through the corridor. A girl and a boy, both in their early years, emerged, rubbing their sleepy eyes. With their unkempt hair and pajama-clad bodies, they appeared to be between four and six years old.

The little boy stood with blonde locks falling across his forehead. His hazel eyes glimmered—a medley of gold and green, flecked with mischief. Rocket pajamas blurred as he tiptoed around her legs, hiding a crayon drawing behind his back. He laughed uncontrollably.

The young boy pointed at him and asked, "Who's he?" almost shouting.

Lucia crouched beside him and patted him tenderly. "This is one of my old friends. He's just stopping by."

The little girl leaned into Lucia's hip, silent. Dark brown eyes tracked him without blinking, her thumb worrying at the seam of her sleeve.

A wisp of a child, her dark hair tumbled in soft, untamed ripples around a face too solemn for her years. Her eyes, fathomless and dark as a moonless night, fixed on him with a subdued intensity that felt like an unspoken verdict. Not a word passed her lips, but her presence alone was an unyielding statement. She did not frown nor scowl, yet her steady, unwavering gaze reflected her disapproval—piercing, impenetrable, and utterly complete. The silence stretched, a chasm of judgment from which no escape seemed possible. She played the part of protector well.

He chuckled, his heart melting at the sight of the children, finding humor in their contrasting natures. "Does she talk?" he asked Lucia, kneeling to their level. "I'm kind of hungry. You guys hungry?" He tried to score friendly points.

The boy's eyes lit up with excitement. "Mac & Cheese!" he exclaimed. The girl remained motionless, while the boy dashed into the kitchen, disappearing.

Lucia laughed falsely, but the smile quickly vanished as she shook her head. "I just got them to go to bed. I'm not so sure you should—"

Her sentence trailed off as his eyes met hers with a smile, but he sensed something broken. He felt compelled to fight through the tension, obsessed with restoring the way things used to be.

He could not help but observe the situation. They entered the kitchen, and he reached for the bowls without being asked; she passed him the spoons. For a moment, it felt practiced, but that moment had already passed. The world had ended.

Just as he was about to inquire about the little boy's whereabouts, a black cat entered the room, purring wildly and rubbing against his legs.

"Jersey!" he exclaimed, picking up the cat and feeling a wave of joy wash over him. Jersey, no longer a kitten, vibrated contentedly in his arms, and he couldn't help but smile at their reunion.

Lucia placed her hand softly on the little girl's neck, motioning for everyone to sit down. She began rummaging through cabinets for late-night snack options. He and the little girl sat at the round kitchen table, the little boy presumably in an extended pantry area, still out of sight. They formed an imperfect symbolic family of four, one that would never be fully realized. The little girl remained emotionless, never taking her eyes off him.

"Why are you here?" Lucia asked suddenly, her tone shifting to one of breathless annoyance as she continued facing the cabinetry. "I don't think you should be here."

He sighed, gently setting Jersey down. "I just wanted to...," he said softly, "... to see you. To see how you were doing."

Lucia's face softened for a moment, but her frustration quickly returned. "You can't just show up out of the blue like this," she said, her voice rising slightly. "You left, remember? You didn't say a word when I needed you the most."

He looked down, guilt and regret etched on his face. "I know, and I'm sorry. I didn't know what to say."

Lucia slammed a cabinet door shut and turned to face him, her eyes blazing. "Last week, I told you I loved you again, and you still didn't say it back. Do you have any idea how much that hurt?"

His heart sank as he vividly recalled those moments. "I was scared. I didn't want to hurt you more."

Meanwhile, the six-year-old girl fussed with the salt and pepper shakers on the table, showing no concern for the quarrel around her. Lucia shook her head, her eyes filling with tears. "Name my newts."

He stared at her, confused. "What? Your newts?"

"Yes!" she snapped. "If you paid any attention, you would know their names. I told you this repeatedly; it's proof you don't care about me at all. Name them!"

He stammered, recalling that the topic had indeed arisen many times. There were three of them she had as pets when she was young—this he was sure—but he could never remember the name of that third lizard. "Wayne NEWTon and Olivia NEWTon-John."

Lucia's face twisted with irritation and sadness. "Keep going. I swear to God, I've told you so many times."

Before he could respond, the little boy burst into the room, holding an open box of instant macaroni and cheese in one hand and a pot in the other. In a fit of playful frustration, he screamed at the top of his lungs, "Mac and Cheese!" Purposefully hitting himself in the forehead with the empty pot, he fell backward onto the ground. Lucia rushed to tend to him, calming him down and ensuring he was okay. The boy lay there laughing hysterically, unharmed.

"Please, just go," she said softly, her back to him as she comforted the boy. "Take Jersey with you. She always liked you better anyway."

Something cinched under his ribs. He tried to swallow but couldn't. His hands went numb around the cat. "I'm sorry," he said. "Truly."

He said nothing more before stepping outside into the darkness, burdened by the weight of his mistakes. A small comfort amidst the chaos, Jersey purred in his arms. As he stepped outside, the coolness of the night air enveloped him. Glancing back at the home, he saw the light from the windows stark against the chilly emptiness. With a deep breath, he moved forward, each step away from the deep black door feeling heavier than the last.

Any semblance of warmth vanished the moment he passed through the entrance. On this cold autumn night, the world was cloaked in a melancholy hush. The air was sharp as shattered glass, biting against his skin as he wandered alone through a concrete forest draped in evening's deepening shadow. The brittle crunch of fallen leaves whispered faded promises beneath his hesitant steps.

The city trees, skeletal and stripped of their splendor, stretched their barren limbs, reaching for something they could never grasp. A chill wind wove through the empty branches, carrying the faint, bittersweet scent of decay. He pulled his coat tighter, though it did little to shield him from the frost that stemmed not from the night but from the aching void within his chest.

Every star above seemed impossibly distant, their faint, flickering light indifferent to his silent grief. The world felt vast and unyielding— loneliness mirrored. In the distance, the mournful cry of an owl cut through the stillness, a sound so hauntingly human that it drew a lump to his throat. He paused, his breath a fleeting mist dissipating into the indifferent air.

Time felt suspended as his mind raced through the deserted streets. He ended up in the park where they used to stroll. Park nights once ended at the all-night diner—her cold hands wrapped around a chipped mug, vapor rising into her hair. He could almost hear the spoon ring against the cup.

Jersey curled up on his lap as he sat on a metal bench. He listened to the motor-like whirr while caressing the ebony cat, rehearsing a conversation with Lucia aloud for her to hear.

"I should have said it back," he muttered. "I should have told her I love her, too. But that word, it—"

Jersey gave a gentle mewl, interrupting him with her own solace. He glanced up at the stars with a weak smile, looking to the sardonic moon peering through clouds, almost expecting an answer. "How did it get this bad?"

It hung pitted and bright—an old shield with too many dents. He wondered how much debris the moon had blocked on behalf of Earth, saving them from peril either by heroism or mere happenstance of its orbit. *No one will ever know what it's done for us.*

As he sat there, he thought about the newts. He couldn't shake the poetic simplicity of remembering the name of a pet salamander. The constant test of this simplistic nature meant nothing to him, yet symbolized everything to her. Guilt-ridden, he admitted to himself that it showed how much he'd taken for granted.

A tear started to form but never fell from his eye. Without his companion, he might have sunk his face into his hands. Instead, he mustered a bit of humor to move forward, looking into his furry friend's eyes. "How am I going to own a cat in a fucking fraternity house?"

Chapter Seven

A Dark Alley

Sheets of rain fell relentlessly, turning the city into a sodden mess of blinking lights and hazy reflections. His breath came in sharp gasps as he ran through the wet streets, each step creating puddles that mirrored the tumultuous environment. Amid the jumble of distorted shapes and sounds that comprised the cityscape, one thing rang clear: the sound of sirens. With each passing second, their wail grew closer and louder, rumbling down the winding streets. The freezing rain felt like tiny needles on his skin, each drop piercing with a keen edge that bordered on anguish. His clothes were drenched and clung to his body, making every step feel laborious. He couldn't slow down; they would arrest him.

He tore through the dark streets, his body moving instinctively as his legs pounded harder. The only thing that mattered was getting away. There was no time to contemplate or understand what was happening. As he ran, the burn in his legs morphed into something else—cold clarity in his joints and a widening pressure behind his eyes. He moved faster than he ever had.

He sensed the fearful eyes of the crowd on him. Faces tipped toward him and then away. A woman yanked a child to her hip. Phones wavered, some dropping, as if reality itself had lifted.

Around the corner, a police vehicle screamed, its headlights harsh against the drenched night. He felt the rays of light pursuing him. His heart hammered in his chest—not just from exertion but from a profound inner shift. It was something more horrifying than sheer adrenaline. It was familiar.

Confusion and terror whirled in his mind, memories racing through his consciousness in a disorganized haze. Intense flashbacks blurred the line between past and present. He ran across the city in these memories, but instead of the streets, he ran beside Lucia along the Schuylkill River as he had months ago, their laughter mingling with the sound of falling water. The sun had shone, and the air had been pleasant that day, filled with the scent of blooming flowers. The picture wavered, warped, and darkened before he returned to the present, his cheeks burning from the chilly rain.

"Lucia..." he whispered while wheezing, his voice lost in the wind and rain. His mental stability wavered; the line between certainty and delusion grew thinner with each step. He could see her and hear her words as though she were running beside him.

"What are you doing?" her voice echoed in his mind—soft, gentle, filled with the tenderness he so desperately craved. "You're running again. You'll find me at the bridge," she continued.

He shook his head, trying to dispel the illusion. With every step, Lucia's ghostly image flickered in and out of existence as he mumbled, "I'll find you."

Her voice and touch were so vivid, so real. The synchronized splash of oars and grunts from rowers in boats charging down the river beside them. Memories bled into the present—another torturous trick his mind was playing, yet he still fell for it. He embraced it.

The sun danced over the Schuylkill River in his mind, scattering diamonds across its rippling surface, while the air droned with the energy of life in motion. Jogging along the winding path, they wove through a tapestry of autumn-hued trees framing the riverbank, their leaves fluttering like applause in the breeze.

Crew rowers glided gracefully over the water, their oars slicing the liquid mirror with synchronized precision, leaving soft, swirling trails in their wake. The rhythmic splash of the blades blended with the distant murmur of city life, creating a symphony of urban serenity as they continued their morning run.

The scent of humid soil and the occasional bloom lingered, mingling with the faint aroma of morning coffee from passing strollers. Joggers nodded in mindful camaraderie, sharing a collective moment of peace and vitality, as if the river itself breathed life into all who came near.

Above, a cloudless sky stretched infinitely blue, embracing the city's skyline peeking beyond the trees, while sunlight filtered through branches, dappling the trail in warm light. It was a day that felt eternal, a perfect blend of motion, nature, and the eased poetry of humanity.

Then, rain knifed through it. The blue shattered, and she was gone. Suddenly—clarity. He stopped and pulled a device with a broken screen from his pocket. He had Mark's phone. He scrolled to her name, his breath caught, and his fingers shook. *Lucia.* He hit the call button without hesitation, and as he ran again, the phone rang in his ear.

Pick up... pick up. His heart pounded. It went unanswered. The ringing faded, overpowered by the rain and sirens. His breath seized in his throat, and for an instant, he thought he would pass out in the middle of the street.

As hopelessness descended, he continued to move forward, propelled by his legs. He hesitated, unsure of what to say as the phone went to voicemail.

He winced at the cracked screen—Mark's number would show on hers.

"Lucia, it's me. I've got Mark's phone. Call back—please. I just need to know you're okay."

The truth shattered him as he held the phone to his ear, unable to utter another word before ending the call. He noted the corner of his mouth attempting to curl into a smile at the thought that at least she would hear his voice one last time—at the very least.

Police cruisers, with their sirens and flashing lights, drew closer. His pulse raced as he scanned for a way out. He cut into an alley—wet brick, a rank gutter, dumpsters hulking like parked trucks. At the end, chain-link caught the streetlight in a dull grid. There was nowhere else to go.

"Freeze!" a voice shouted from behind him, rough and authoritative. He spun around, hands raised instinctively, heart racing as he faced the officer who had cornered him.

A middle-aged Black officer stood, badge bright, gun ready—a thin gold cross glinting at his collar. He recognized the voice from the fountain.

"Hands up! Don't move!"

A wave of panic surged through him, his mind racing to find the words that would make the officer understand. The policeman had a lean but athletic build, symbolizing discipline and readiness for his duties. His dark skin and face conveyed a mix of youthful energy and mature responsibility, with a neatly maintained fade reflecting professionalism and a trimmed beard contributing to an approachable respect that radiated from him.

His eyes were notably deep and insightful, shining with an empathetic intensity capable of communicating both firmness and compassion. His uniform was complete, with a badge prominently displayed on his chest and a belt carrying the essential tools of the trade.

"Please," he gasped to the officer, his voice trembling with desperation. "I need to find her. She's in danger... we're all in danger."

The officer's eyes softened slightly. A flicker of recognition crossed his face as he said, "Look, son. My name is John. I don't know what's going on, but you need to calm down and do as I say. We just need to know what's been happening today. We need to talk. Do not put your hands down."

"You don't understand!" he cried, stepping forward, hands trembling. "This is... the end of everything."

John's grip on his revolver tightened, but there was still hesitation in his stance, a moment of doubt hanging in the air between them.

"I was there earlier today when—just put your hands on top of your head and let me cuff you. We can talk; we can make sense of what's going on here," the officer professed, his voice now relaxed, almost gentle.

Training warred with curiosity. "Tell me what's going on," he insisted.

"It's them," he whispered to John. "The angels... only, they're something else. They're here to end it all."

John's brow furrowed, confusion and concern mingling in his expression. "What are you talking about? Son, you need to—"

Out on the avenue, sirens rose and fell, sliding past. John glanced toward the mouth of the alley—no backup. He was torn between instinct and a desire to understand the catastrophic events plaguing his city.

"Please, John," he begged, voice breaking. "You must believe me. They're coming for all of us. I have to find her... there is almost no time left."

The officer looked back at him; his eyes filled with a mix of pity and resolve. "I don't know what's going on, but I can't let you go. You need to just come with me."

Desperation clawed at his chest, and he glanced at the fence behind him— *the only way out*. "I'm sorry," he whispered, taking a step back. "I have to get to her."

Without warning, he turned and leapt at the fence, fingers gripping the cold metal as he began to climb. "Stop!" John shouted, panic in his voice. "Don't do this! I will open fire!"

The rain continued to beat down on him as he climbed, his breath coming in short gasps. A gunshot cut through the darkness like a blade, just as he grabbed the top bar, ready to clear to the other side. With horrified eyes, he slowly climbed back down and froze, pulse pounding as he stared through the chain-link fence.

The officer stood stiffened, his revolver still smoking. They both looked down at the unimaginable. The bullet, flattened at the tip, dropped harmlessly into a puddle of filthy rain.

Gazing at the projectile, his thoughts reeled from the sheer absurdity of it all. Thick sheets of rain fell around him, icy water splattering into the puddle where the bullet lay, creating swirls that mocked the entire situation. In the faint light of the alley, the flattened bullet shone dully— an unthinkable defiance of fate and physics.

His gaze shifted from the bullet to the officer, whose expression reflected terror and confusion. John seemed unable to process what had just happened; wide eyes and slightly open lips betrayed his disbelief. His confidence in authority and strength vanished in an instant, leaving the gun trembling in his hands.

The rain continued to pour, dripping from their chins, streaming down their faces, soaking through their clothes.

The chill had left him. Everything felt clear again. He managed to control his breathing. Even while aware of every detail—the rain, the darkness, the fear in the officer's eyes—it all felt disconnected, as if happening to someone else. He looked back at the officer slowly, his expression subdued, almost peaceful. In response, the cop felt a shiver of serene conviction rather than fury or fear.

Run.

He stared at John, quiet and absolute, who took two steps back without breaking eye contact; the muzzle dipped slightly. The alley listened.

The officer's face filled with dread and confusion as he hesitated after hearing the instruction. John's heart skipped a beat. Something in the officer's eyes and the way he uttered that single word suggested he knew something dreadful awaited on the other side of the chain link.

John retreated a step. In that moment, despite the rain still falling and sirens wailing in the distance, the only sound the cop could hear was the loud, furious pounding of his own heart. They stood together, waiting in the wet darkness for what was to come.

As the downpour washed away the blood and dread, the officer glanced at the flattened piece of ammunition one last time, keeping his head down— a sobering reminder of the forces at work. The air thickened. A heavy, rhythmic gust raked the fence—wingbeats big enough to move rain.

The alley seemed to hold its breath. The bullet lay still, a solemn echo of violence spent. Its once-pristine form, now marred and warped, glinted faintly under the soft moonlight, bearing the hidden scars of its journey. The surface was dark, as if it absorbed shadows, its edges frayed yet defiant—telling tales of power unleashed and force met. A relic of fleeting fury.

Chapter Eight

A Tourniquet

Rain tapped his collar; brick cooled his spine. Then the doorway opened again—sunlit afternoon, Lucia's smile, a black kitten trembling in his hands.

"Surprise!" he exclaimed, excitement and nervousness mingling in his voice.

He'd been planning for weeks, knowing how much she adored cats. Her face made all the effort worthwhile—shock, happiness, and a smile that lit up the space.

She laughed, eyes glistening. "What did you do?" The tiny creature mewed and shivered in her hands as he handed it over. She held it gently, cupping it as she stroked its soft coat.

"For us," he replied, his heart swelling with affection as he looked at her. "I figured we needed some company around here." A peal of pure, unadulterated laughter filled the room as Lucia, emotionally overcome, sniffled.

"I love it. And I love you," she whispered, her gaze shifting to the kitten, now purring serenely in her arms.

"What should we name her?"

For the next several minutes, they batted around ideas. Then Lucia looked up with a playful glint in her eyes.

"Jersey," she said.

"What, after the state?"

"Yeah, kind of. Where the shelter was and what we always stare at from the bench along the river."

He laughed, shaking his head.

"Uhh, Jersey it is," he confirmed, leaning over to place a soft kiss on her forehead. The kitten, now officially named, curled up in her lap, purring louder. The afternoon blurred into a joyful mix of lounging on the couch, talking, and playing with their furry companion. They hardly noticed the world outside. It was a simple afternoon where hours felt like mere minutes. Recalling it now filled him with an enormous, fiery warmth—a cherished memory from a dark, disgusting alleyway.

They set out the food, water, litter box, and toys, then reluctantly left the apartment for one of their ritual walks, leaving the cat alone for the first time aching their hearts. After about an hour of walking through sought-after places, they arrived at their favorite spot, gazing up at the Ben Franklin Bridge, its steel beams glinting in the sunlight. They found their bench.

The bridge rose like a steel cathedral over their pew, pale blue towers standing patient against the sky. Cables fell like harp strings, humming with traffic. Sunlight slid along the lattice, making the river blink. At night, dotted lights hung like a low constellation. They always felt small here. The bridge—a part of their story.

The city stretched behind them, a landscape of urban architecture framed by mossy greenish waterways, with the sky sprawling above. Lucia sat by his side, her hand slipping into his as they gazed at the view of Camden in the distance.

"Love this spot," she said softly, wistfulness in her voice. "So peaceful here."

He nodded, gently squeezing her hand. "Yes, it is," he whispered, his tone soft like a forgotten memory. He was so happy here.

"I love you," she said, eyes unguarded.

His mouth opened—stalled. Only the traffic spoke for what felt like an eternity.

"Let me grab us some slices," he blurted. "Two minutes. Don't move."

His heart skipped a beat, the weight of her words settling over him. He tried to reply, wanting to say the words, but they stuck in his throat, fear holding them back. Her smile faltered, eyes searching his for reassurance. He couldn't bring himself to say it—could not admit that he was scared, that he wasn't sure he could ever give her what she needed.

She blinked, then found a smile. "Sure."

He felt a stab of guilt as he turned away and jogged toward the pizza shop. He grabbed the door handle and pulled it open, the bell ringing above him to notify the shopkeeper. He didn't fully enter when a distant crash echoed through the air, followed by shouts. His head snapped up, eyes scanning for the source of the commotion, fear coiling in his stomach.

A weld flash from the steel girders nearby. Then the wrong kind of groan. Yells pierced the air as the beam shifted, hanging crooked. His stomach dropped. Metal tearing. No sound came.

He lunged. The air kicked him sideways—then dust, metal screaming, ears ringing. He clawed forward, eyes stinging. The shockwave threw him off balance. He scrambled to his feet, trying to find Lucia through the fog of debris, his heart in his throat. The steel behemoth swayed, then landed, and the piercing scream of his lover cut through the cloud.

"No, no, no…" he whispered, fear gripping his chest as he ran and dropped to the ground beside her. "Lucia, please… Oh my God." The horrified screams of passersby echoed around them.

Blood pooled around her leg, where the beam had impacted—purple. Something cold pressed behind his eyes; the world narrowed to her leg. He got both hands under the beam and heaved. It sailed away, vanished with a distant splash. The crowd, once inching forward, now stepped back in awe and confusion.

His hands trembled as he screamed at the onlookers.

"Someone help! HELP!" Tears streamed down his face, pupils now dilated, pits of night.

A voice began to speak. He looked around but couldn't find the source. A familiar voice, coming from somewhere near.

Higher, above the wound. Tight—but not dead.

He stripped off his shirt, hands shaking, and cinched it in place.

He followed the instructions given, instructions no one else could hear.

Her faint cries, full of unconscious anguish, made his pulse race as he hesitated, then squeezed the makeshift tourniquet.

"I'm sorry," he whispered, a single tear falling onto her belly, his voice breaking. "I have to do this, or he says we'll lose the leg."

Lucia gave him a confused look, then let out a bellowing screech. He watched her leg swell, turning a deep violet as blood pooled beneath the skin. He understood immediately—the leg would be lost unless he acted swiftly. The thought of her enduring such an injury—the thought of her losing a part of herself—cut at his soul.

"Please... someone help us!" he shouted again, his voice raw with desperation. No horns. Just a plastic bag skittering along the curb as if it had somewhere to be.

He tightened the tourniquet, his hands slick with blood, until her breath hitched and the flow slowed.

"Stay with me," he whispered, his voice trembling. "Please."

The sound of sirens grew louder, piercing the air. A wave of relief mixed with anxiety inundated him. *Don't take her.*

In a flurry of flashing lights and hurried steps, the paramedics arrived and rushed to Lucia's side. They checked her vitals, prepared her for transport.

One paramedic glanced at the knot as she snipped gauze. "Good job on that tourniquet—you may have saved her leg."

The reality of what he had done sank in, the weight of it both a relief and a heavy burden. The mysterious voice in his head—it all felt unreal.

"Will she be okay?" he asked, his voice barely above a murmur as he watched them lift Lucia onto a stretcher.

The paramedic looked at him, maintaining professionalism but with a hint of kindness. "She's in critical condition, but you saved her. We need to get her to the ER right away."

As adrenaline faded, his legs buckled, and he collapsed onto the slick ground, trembling with guilt. A gentle touch on his shoulder pulled him back from the brink of despair.

"Come on," the paramedic said. "Let's get you checked out too."

His vision blurred, the world spinning as exhaustion overwhelmed him. His heart pounded as he numbly followed the paramedic, moving on autopilot. When they loaded Lucia into the ambulance, he climbed in after her, desperate to stay close. He gripped her cold, clammy hand, as if his touch could keep her tethered to life.

He faced the inside of the vehicle, staring at the red lever that locked them in. With the night darkening, he looked upward through the door's tiny window. The moon cast a bluish hue over the sky, which had not yet turned completely black. He stared at the shrill, sapphire-lit grin and felt, absurdly, that it was both mocking him and keeping watch.

The ride was a terrifying blur of flashing lights and sirens, the outside world a cacophony of noise. All he could focus on was Lucia, watching her chest rise and fall with shallow, labored breaths. It had been so long since he'd prayed; now his pleas were silent, sheepishly directed toward any higher power willing to listen. He felt like a hypocrite, having strayed from any semblance of religion long ago.

Please... I'll do anything.

At last, the lights of the hospital emerged, a sharp contrast to the night's gloom. She was hurried inside. He staggered out of the vehicle, attempting to follow them, but his vision blurred again.

As the gurney turned, two syllables slipped from under her mask—*the bridge*—or maybe it was the squeak of a wheel. He reached for the word anyway.

Inside, striving to follow her as she rolled further away, he was suddenly overcome with exhaustion. Everything dimmed, and as the sound of shouting grew louder, the voices spun faster. Cold gloves found his wrist. Fluorescents hummed like insects. *Don't take her from me.*

Chapter Nine

A Fair Fight

The tension of the night clung to him as he walked past the officer, down the alleyway and into the street. John lowered his revolver and let him pass. Still soaked from the downpour that had subsided, he noted they were close to the horrific battle that had taken place only hours earlier. He stared up helplessly at the office building leaning against the adjacent high-rise it had crashed into.

The lofty marvel of steel and glass, once proud and vertical, now leaned as if surrendering to gravity's pull. Its sleek facade, once rigid, curved gracefully toward its taller neighbor—a lookout that rose with unwavering authority. The building rested upon it like a weary traveler seeking refuge, the two structures forming an intimate embrace, their silhouettes woven together against the sky. The angled glass windows caught the light in an almost wistful dance, refracting the colors of the glowing moon as if to celebrate their newfound union. Below, the street vibrated with the soft tremor of their unexpected connection, as if the city held its breath, marveling at the delicate balance they had found in this strange, poetic repose of destruction.

His senses heightened. The world slowed. His steady footsteps and breathing were the only sounds as the city's hum waned. Straight overhead, a figure emerged—large, winged flaps, landing in the middle of the street close to where the day's nightmare began.

Feathered extensions tucked behind its back, the tall, powerful form exuded confidence. It was the same angelic figure as before, now surrounded by a faint glow. He felt a cold amusement in the way it watched him—the universe dimmed just to give them space. *Its version of respect, he defeated its kin twice.*

In the city's epicenter, where the silent purr of life mingled with the whispers of forgotten souls, it stood—beautiful and terrible in equal measure. Wings limewashed, shimmered with a haunting, otherworldly shine. The light they cast was cold, and within its gaze lingered an obscurity that bent the air.

It held still, its presence as quiet as the fall of night—stillness vibrated with the weight of endless time. A sick joke. A choice of costume to instill fear in the insects it decided to remove from its new home.

It is almost over.

The words landed without a sound, a cool heaviness behind his eyes.

He took a moment to reply, his heart racing from a mix of fear and courage. The strength in his limbs, the same energy that had carried him through the streets earlier, was still there. He was ready.

"Yes," he finally said, his voice steady. He chose to verbalize a response rather than send the thought directly into the mind of his opponent. "I'm done running. This time, give me a sword."

The figure regarded him with a hint of curiosity, eager to outperform its cloned brethren that had failed before it.

The fraudulently cherubic figure held up a hand. A long, sharp blade flashed in the low light and materialized, as if tearing through time and space to land in its palm.

He then raised his own hand, and sure enough, an identical weapon appeared. He gripped it firmly, not pausing to ponder why it felt so good in his grasp. He simply knew this was his tool—in this moment—his way to stop the madness and continue toward the end of the world.

The foreign sword buzzed softly as it settled into his grip, its weight a gentle burden, remembering forgotten wars. The grip, carved from metal that gleamed with an unearthly shimmer, cooled his fingers. Beneath its surface pulsed a heat—a steady, ancient heartbeat of ages long past.

The blade was unnaturally light, impossibly sharp. His senses tingled, the sword not just an instrument—a conduit. His thudding veins quickened, and for a moment, he was no longer mortal, but an extension of the sword's eternal will. The blade sang softly in the air, an ancient song carried on the wind, reminding him that he was both its master and its slave.

With a shimmer of transcendental light, the opponent moved to a starting position. They faced one another, tension in their postures, and the air thickened before action—steel clashed.

He parried high, slid along the wing's shadow, and stepped off-line. The creature cut low; he rolled, coming up slicing for ribs. Sparks leapt. Breathe. Move. With each swing of his sword, he moved with startling accuracy and speed, driven by an unknown force. With equal dexterity, its form moved, each blow designed to end the conflict.

He was determined not to give in. With all his force and will—retaliation, sending sparks flying as his sword slashed across the figure's twin weapon. He ignored the pain in his lungs and the strain in his muscles, concentrating solely on the fight.

He noticed a gap. The angel paused, its head slightly bowed. Seizing the chance, he unleashed a powerful blow. The figure's defenses crumbled under the sword's true strike, leaving a serious wound on its side. The normally expressionless adversary staggered back, astonishment etched on its face. Even if it was a minor triumph, it was still a victory. He pressed forward, fueled by fresh vigor.

Wind churned the dust sideways; a broad shadow swept the street. Steel hissed past his ear. *Another one.* There was no time to think—this one moved so quickly it took him by surprise, its blade slicing through the air with lethal precision.

The two angels flanked him—one high, one low—herding him onto the curb. He hopped the centerline, blade catching on a fender and ringing his wrist. *Don't get pinned. Keep the sword.* Breath thinned; arms shook.

Amid the chaos, he noticed. Their blades kissed and slid—an instant of crossed momentum. It was enough. He drove straight through the seam and shouldered them apart.

The first stumbled, losing its balance, but it did not hesitate. He moved quickly and struck again, his blade finding its mark. The creature gasped in pain as the sword pierced its chest, hurtling to the ground. The black in its eyes receded like ink in water, hazel surfacing around the pupil. The wing shivered once then fell still.

Stunned and enraged by its companion's death, the other unleashed a vicious assault. Every blow in the rancorous swordfight was more powerful than the last. He would not lose to the soulless. He deflected a hard blow and swung his sword with intent. The angel was caught off guard as the blade broke through its layers of defense and into its side. With a howl of agony, it staggered back, wings wavering.

The next hit spun him; sweat and grit burned his eyes. He reset his grip— found his feet.

The figure lunged at him with sword raised, but this time he was ready. With quick, precise movements, he sidestepped the attack and used all his remaining power to drive his sword forward. The blade punctured the assailant's chest.

The imposter released a final, gasping breath, its wings spread wide, eyes amplifying in shock. Then, like the first, it collapsed to the ground, energy fading as its body hemorrhaged. The chest light blew out, dark ink spattering the pavement. Rain beaded along the feathers, running black.

He stood there, sword still raised, his chest heaving from the effort of the fight. *No enemies remained.*

The only sounds were his steady heartbeat and the faint buzz of the city in the distance.

As the wind carried away the last traces of dust from the scuffle, a wave of exhaustion washed over him. He stood alone in the darkness, burdened by the weight of what he had done. The sword he held faded into nothingness.

He did not feel the sensation of losing consciousness as before. He was stronger now. The fight was over—a distraction from the mission he was committed to.

He turned and began to walk, casting one last glance at the spot where angels had fallen. They must have started to evacuate the city—there was not a soul in sight, in any direction.

He found himself once more in the middle of Broad Street, an empty vein stretching through the city's silent heart. The street, once a pulse of movement, now lay still, a dark ribbon beneath the weight of the sky. Streetlights flickered like distant stars, casting a pale glow on the cracked pavement, where shadows stretched long and thin, clawing at the edges of the world. The buildings loomed like prehistoric watchmen, cold and indifferent, their windows like hollow eyes staring into the abyss. No whir of traffic, no mutter of voices—just the deep breath of the city, lost in its own forgotten hours. The air hung heavy with silence, and the wind whispered secrets he could not discern as it swept through the empty alleys. Time bent here, caught in the suspended moment between dusk and dawn. The city stood as a monument to its own solitude.

Though his body was worn, his determination remained firm. He would find Lucia. He finally noticed the officer who had witnessed the entire encounter from the alleyway where they had met. John stood with his hands open, rain glistening on his cap.

"Go home, John. Be with the people you care about. By morning, this will all be gone," he said, jogging east without looking back.

Chapter Ten

A Snowy Cab Ride

The billiard hall's warm glow served as a comfortable haven from the cold outside. The night was filled with laughter and the sound of clicking pool balls. Dim amber light pulsed through the space, casting shadows on the worn felt of the tables.

The air was thick with the murmur of youthful voices, laughter spilling over drinks sloshing in vibrant cups against the dark wood of the bar. A jukebox sang proudly from the back, the bass reverberating through the room and vibrating the floor beneath every footstep. Young students, faces flushed with the passion of their drinks and the excitement of the game, leaned in with competitive fire, their cue sticks like extensions of their hands. Each crack of a ball was sharp and sweet, a fleeting moment of focus amidst the beautiful chaos.

A thin fog of cold air drifted in each time the door opened, smearing the light above their heads and blending with the notes of a familiar song. Time slowed as the night stretched on, the room alive with laughter, clinking glass, and deep tunes that wrapped the world in their carefree embrace.

With emotions light and smiles easy, he and Lucia were tucked into the noise, calm and deep. He forgot his watch existed. Even the door's cold rush faded to a hush at their backs.

They hadn't been out many times, but tonight she slid her hand inside his sleeve to warm her fingers. He couldn't stop smiling. They had gathered with friends for laid-back evenings that didn't require any preparation, but this one felt particularly memorable. The atmosphere was lively, with people taking turns at the billiard table and engaging in pleasant games mixed with anecdotes, shots of whiskey, and too much beer.

"Hey, how did you two meet, anyway?" Matthew asked, anxiously glancing between them with a grin, his arm around both.

He and Lucia exchanged a look, both smiling, but then a slight frown crossed his face. The truth—the exact moment they had met—was blurry, forgotten. It wasn't grasped as a grand event; instead, it was a series of small encounters that had gradually drawn them together. *A piece was missing.*

With everyone waiting for an answer, he composed a response.

"Uh... Econ-101? Or the hallway outside, I guess?" He laughed helplessly. "I'm not sure."

"We kept bumping into each other until we figured it out," Lucia rescued, her eyes lit.

There was a faint understanding between them as their friends laughed, and the moment vanished. The fact they couldn't remember mattered little. They were together right now. Matthew, Luke, and the others stepped back to give the two lovers space and headed toward the bar.

The familiar music began to play on the jukebox hanging on the wall as the night went on. The gentle tones of The Cure's *Just Like Heaven* enveloped them in the welcoming embrace of the space. Two words—*you... you*—and the rest of the room fell away.

Lucia reclined against the pool table, her gaze drifting from the game to the music, which caught his attention. Her lips formed a gentle smirk, and for an instant, all else faded. It was just the two of them and the song— happiness, nostalgia, and a touch of melancholy.

"I love this song," Lucia said softly, her voice barely audible over the melody. "It always makes me feel... like everything is exactly as it was meant to be."

He nodded. Even while the outer world felt chaotic and unexpected, he was forced to admit there were times when everything seemed to fall into place. It was almost miraculous how the music, the room's temperature growing warmer, and the presence of the person he cared for came together.

"What if heaven's just... floating? Like, we become clumps of energy in a lava lamp?" he asked, prompted by the lyrics they heard.

"What?" She welcomed the intro but disguised her intrigue as shock.

"Seriously," he added. "Whatever life force powers our bodies right now... and they say energy can never truly be destroyed, only transferred. Then it, we, must go somewhere."

"Okay, so... that means we're destined to drift aimlessly in the afterlife."

He chuckled, realizing how his idea must have sounded, and how the deepest of conversations was occurring prematurely on a third date. He paused, feeling incredible comfort in sharing hopes and fears.

"Well. Maybe we're allowed to take our memories with us."

She stared into his eyes now, silently and therapeutically playing the role of audience.

"I... it's just that I had this dream once. It was a train. I was in the front car. Another train charged straight at us—white lights, no brakes. In the dream, I died. The vivid fear was that there was nothing but darkness. Just pure nothingness," he continued.

She saw true distress sparkle across his slightly glassy hazel eyes.

"Okay, um," she piled on. "Well then, metaphorically. As you're floating through the cold, dark parts of your lava lamp theory... maybe every 8 billion years or so, you clash with a whirling glob of someone else. Then, as you sort of temporarily mold with them... things get a little less dark—a little less cold."

"Better than nothing," he concluded, then took a series of chugs from his beer.

She finished her drink and signaled that it was time to leave. They stopped again, returning to consciousness, and remained silent to experience the chorus of the song that came back into focus from the speakers.

The enormous crowd around them was back now, having never left. Realizing they had been in their own little world, they both agreed—without verbalizing it—that it was time to sneak out undetected. Mark then joyously appeared, holding shots of brown liquor for everyone to partake in.

The three clinked their tiny glasses together. The shot of whiskey was like a secret whispered into his soul. It slid smooth and slow, curling in its amber heat as it settled deep within, igniting a fire with the first kiss of its bite. The liquid carried the essence of the earth—smoky oak, a tinge of vanilla, a trace of sweet caramel—folded into the deep notes of aged wood and rich barley. As it swirled down, it lingered on the tongue, a dance of subtle syrupiness before its warmth spread like sunlight on a cold morning—soft and steady. Its embrace, both bold and tender, left the taste of memory on their lips.

"This guy's the greatest," Mark slurred, slinging an arm around him. "I'm gonna be president just like he was—watch."

Mark looked to Luke, who tipped his chin once in quiet agreement.

As Mark and Luke became enthralled in a new conversation, Lucia looked deep into his eyes and tilted her head, signaling for an escape.

They slipped out the double doors. Outside, the snow swallowed sound; the music inside thumped to a distant blur. Snow lay clean and thick over the buried curb. A yellow cab idled alone; the wipers kept time—thup, thup, thup.

He felt nervous now; he had waited to relive this moment for such a long time. He lifted his head upward toward the sky, where a break in the clouds revealed the moon, ever smiling. It hung low, a beautiful crescent that brought back memories of both the past and the present.

"Look at that," he said, pointing. "It's like the cat from *Alice in Wonderland*."

Lucia followed his gaze, her eyes lighting up as she recognized the reference. Without missing a beat, she began to recite.

"The moon was shining sulkily..." she continued, reciting an entire section from the British children's book.

Mesmerized and slightly embarrassed, his observation was merely an uneducated reference to a cartoon he vaguely remembered—he folded his mouth downward to feign admiration. "Wow, that's incredible," he replied casually.

"So, um, would you like to come back to my place, even though I just ruined the idea of eternity for you? I promise you'll barely notice the forty fraternity brothers all sleeping under one roof," he said, exuding warmness despite the flurrying snow.

"I'd better not," she replied. "It's better if you come with me to my place."

A shared first kiss followed as indistinct chatter and laughter spilled from the bar doors. He opened the cab door, helped her in, and closed it. Lucia rested her head on his shoulder, gazing out at the snow-covered streets as her breath fogged the window.

"This feels like a dream," she murmured, her voice soft and content. "I don't want it to end."

He wrapped his arm around her, pulling her closer. "Let's just enjoy it right here, right now," he whispered back.

They traveled in silence, low-volume jazz filling the compact cab while snow continued to fall softly outside. They felt safe in this small bubble of affection and music, but then a chill hit them both. They didn't move; in fact, he pulled her tighter. They knew the memory was fading and that they were being pulled apart once more. Reliving this moment was a gift, and heat was only discernible when contrasted with the cold. In unison, without needing to whisper, they closed their eyes tightly.

Chapter Eleven

A 1990 Chevy Camaro

He stared at it in disbelief, tracing the familiar lines of the so-called muscle car resting before him. The deep rumble of the engine still resonated in his mind, a memory from a time when things were simpler, before the world had broken.

A white Camaro—a symphony of steel and spirit—gleamed like frost under the streetlamp, just as the light snapped off in preparation for dawn. Its sharp angles softened by time yet resolute in stance—a prowling panther frozen mid-stride. The paint, a distilled winter storm, held stories of past highways kissed by rain and sun. The bold grille, defiant and smirking, hinted at power coiled beneath the hood—a roar untamed, masked in repose.

Its curves were testosterone-fueled poetry, where muscle met grace, and the era's rebellion was etched in every line.

T-tops invited the heavens in, framing a cockpit of worn leather—a shrine to speed, freedom, and endless asphalt. The car didn't just sit; it waited. He opened the door—it was unlocked.

Relief washed over his face as he found the transportation. His endless running could finally subside, but that peace didn't last. He glanced at the stick shift, and a wave of nostalgia hit him as he remembered Lucia. Images of her teaching him to drive the manual transmission took him to another world. He could still hear her voice, patient and encouraging, guiding him through each gear change in a deserted parking lot that day, her laughter filling the car whenever he stalled the engine. One of those moments, insignificant at the time, had somehow stayed with him.

He inhaled deeply, wiping sweat from his cheeks. The terror that plagued the city earlier had sent people fleeing—or worse. The hazards still ticked, and a red valet tag dangled from the key in the cupholder—someone had abandoned it in a hurry. He inserted the key into the ignition.

The sky was turning from black to purple, signaling dawn's approach. The sound of police sirens grew louder, breaking the tranquility. He needed to escape; the gravity of the situation pressed on him. He glared at the stick shift, recalling lighthearted quarrels with Lucia, when he had insisted there was no need to learn to drive such vehicles in the modern age. He dwelled on the fact that he had no idea how to drive this car. His mouth slightly agape, he stared forward, lost in thought. *I'm trapped.*

The memory of her attempts to train him on their second date surged back—when the car reacted to his touch as he changed gears, forcing her Camaro to make horrific grinding sounds. He could almost imagine her smiling at him, her unwavering faith in him. With everything foreign and out of place, there was a curious comfort in the familiarity of her voice.

The Camaro was real, though. There was an actual stick shift in his hand. It was all genuine: the moisture on his forehead, the thumping in his heart, the dried blood covering his body, and the flashing police lights behind him. The passenger door opened.

Lucia entered and closed the door behind her. "Hey, sweetie," she said, heavily panting. "How are you holding up?"

He didn't answer, keeping his gaze forward, his mouth open, tears threatening to fall.

"Baby, hello? You can't just—" she stopped short when she heard the sirens in the distance.

After a long pause, he finally responded to the apparition. "I've finally snapped, I guess," he said, his voice broken. "I'm going crazy, but I'm not crazy enough to think you're really here."

"I'm not here," she said, glancing down—party-ready top, a black skirt, heels sharp as commas. "Nice outfit for the end of the world, though, right?"

"This means I'm just... I've finally lost it." He buried his head in his bloodied hands. The sirens grew louder. The police were blocks away.

"Okay, we gotta push through, honey. We really gotta get moving," she said, looking back at the police cars stopped close behind them.

"It's a stick shift. I can't... You know I don't know how to—" he whispered, starting to hyperventilate.

"Babe, stop. You know how to drive stick. I taught you," she said, leaning back in her seat, calmly checking her reflection in the mirror. She popped the cap off her deep red lipstick and began applying it to her lips.

"That was months ago, and it didn't exactly go well. I don't remember a single thing," he tried to correct her.

The police cars surrounded them. An officer exited and demanded through his megaphone that he take the key out of the ignition.

"If I know it, sitting here with you right now means you know it. Just listen—we're almost out of time," she said more sternly.

"Where do I find you?" he asked desperately, finally putting his hand on the manual gear shift and looking into the eyes of the young woman who wasn't there.

"You find me at the bridge," she said, locking eyes with him. "Now listen." Everything she said, he simultaneously acted out, as if he knew what to do before she said it.

"Press the brake and the clutch," she instructed, placing her hand over his on the shifter. "Slowly let off the clutch... now push the clutch to the floor... Turn the car on."

He turned the key.

A symphony awoke—a low growl stirring deep in the Camaro's metallic chest, a beast roused from sleep. The guttural rumble cascaded from the automobile, a voice both primal and precise, gritty with echoes of the past.

Its tone was a promise—raw power, restrained for now but always ready to break loose and take him where he needed to be. Each cylinder fired in rhythmic harmony, a heartbeat of steel and pungent gasoline pulsing through the exhaust in throaty waves. The sound swelled, filling the air with memories of bituminous pathways and burnt rubber. Then, the idle— a deep, resonant purr that lingered, steady and certain.

The music started automatically, the sound of giant bass subwoofers booming from the back. Kesha's *Die Young* detonated from the speakers; he flinched and smacked the volume down a notch.

First gear. Ease to the bite—feel it.

Feather the gas. Now lift—smooth.

"Driver, show me your hands! Turn the engine off—now!" shouted the officer.

Fucking floor it!

He slammed his foot down on the gas pedal to her command; the hood of the car lifted off the ground, and the vehicle surged forward. "Now put it in second... now third... Here we go!" she continued, giggling.

Lucia leaned over and kissed his cheek. They tore through the city streets, up the nearby ramp, and onto the highway. The police followed closely but failed to keep up as the intimate knowledge of the city's twists, turns, and gear shifts eluded them.

Each verbal direction provided by the young woman was followed before the instruction was fully uttered. He pressed harder on the gas pedal, sending the car racing forward as he shifted into the next gear, and then the next. As he swerved between lanes, the engine snarled, and the tires gripped the damp road. The city began to fade from view, its buildings and streetlights merging into a blur of multicolored streaks. Dawn was approaching, and the deep purple of the night yielded to the first hints of pink and orange in the sky.

Surroundings became increasingly disorienting. The chase intensified, with more flashing lights appearing in his rearview mirror. Despite the growing chaos, Lucia's voice remained steady—a constant he clung to.

"You're doing great," she said while sporadically humming to the pop song coming through the radio, her voice calm amid the turmoil. "Keep moving forward. We're getting close."

He gained considerable distance and checked his mirrors—something was terribly wrong. Ahead, the bridge rose, its blue steel frame standing in stark contrast to the breaking dawn. A strange mixture of dread and joy washed over him as he beheld it. This was the moment where everything would come to light, and he would finally experience the reunion he had longed for.

On the opposite lanes of the roadway, a series of vehicles passed—trucks and cars—moving with unsettling precision but without drivers.

Eventually, they slowed and collided into one another. No matter how he adjusted his rearview, it reflected only darkness. The same void filled the side mirrors. The wheel felt light in his hands. He glanced over his shoulder—nothing but a matte black swallowing the lanes. He stomped on the brakes and skidded into the divider. Turning to the passenger seat, he found it empty.

He slowly exited the car, the door creaking open with each reluctant inch. He stood in the middle of the highway, alone, with no other vehicle in sight. A wall of pure black cut off the northbound lanes, swallowing light rather than reflecting it. Up close, it appeared lusterless, almost soft-looking, tugging at his shirt like a hidden current. A faint hum resonated within it. He stepped closer and felt a pull in his teeth. Eerie booming sounds emanated from the other side of the colorless barrier.

The blockade moved in his direction, the crashing sounds growing louder until a red, worn pickup truck emerged from the void, its front seat occupied by three playful dogs: a brown German Shepherd-Labrador mix, a pure black Labrador, and a Terrier-Poodle mix, all happily wagging their tails and panting—yet no driver was in sight. More crashes followed as another car emerged from the darkness, then another, also devoid of operator or passenger.

This had to be the point of it—the dogs whining yet safe in the cab. It wasn't everything; it was just *us*. Animals and plant life would remain.

He felt the wall's pull in his bones, an irresistible force drawing him closer. He focused on the dogs to his right, oblivious to the encroaching void, their eyes bright with innocence and joy. Of course they would be spared.

They didn't bargain or brood; they forgave at a glance. In a world unraveling, their enjoyment felt like proof that goodness wasn't extinct. They loved not for gain, but because their hearts overflowed with unclouded, unconditional affection.

A dog's innocence shone through in how they greeted each day as if it were spun from golden threads, how they forgave as easily as a breeze, and how they curled beside you, unquestioning.

He found peace in the thought that his black cat would live on. At sunrise, she'd stretch on a stone wall, then tap a paw into a bright stream of water running along the curb, flicking shiny specs of light into the air. By noon, she'd doze in a cool patch of shade; by afternoon, she'd stalk birds in a wild tangle of weeds. At sunset, she'd watch the runoff burn gold. In time, the memory of him would fade.

Below, a semi-truck began to make a wide turn onto the on-ramp, narrowly avoiding the blackness—belching with every gear change as it ascended the incline. The humming wall remained unseen by the driver.

He glanced at the bridge above, then at the truck ascending to the highway. He started running toward it, then stopped short. With a quick smirk, he turned, opened the car door, and let the dogs out of the passenger door. They sprang toward him, running with frantic sniffs and unbridled excitement, their barking echoing through the deserted road. He gave each of them a final pat, their fur warm and soft beneath his palms. They played with one another, passing in and out of the supernatural black barrier with ease.

He jogged beside the on-ramp wall, timing the rise. *Jump.*

With one running step onto a crash barrier, he landed on the truck's roof, hands burning. He and the vehicle came under the bridge, and he sprang to catch a diagonal girder, boots scraping until a bolt head offered him purchase. Inch by inch, the muscles he had honed over the past months helped him climb the cold metal spans of the bridge. He reached the viaduct's roadway surface.

"Lucia! Lucia!" he screamed. Traffic was frantic on the overpass, with both eastbound and westbound lanes nearly engulfed by darkness. He made his way to the shoulder and ran toward the center. The black wall crept ever closer, moving parallel to the bridge. He turned abruptly, arms falling to his hips, as he noticed a second mirrored wall on the other side. He was now entombed between two black curtains being drawn, destined to converge.

The walls crept closer, lane lines squeezing to a ribbon. A car horn blared in the distance—and cut off mid-note. The sounds of people and traffic faded more and more, becoming total silence.

The comforting, high-pitched guitar riff from *Just Like Heaven* began to play. He gazed at the blackness surrounding him, stunned, trying to determine the source of the music. It was coming from his pocket. Mark's ringtone, with the text "Incoming call: Lucia" displayed across the screen.

He drew a breath and held it.

"Hello?" he said, his voice calm but shaky, somehow smiling in the chaos.

"Oh my god, what's going on? Are you okay?" she asked, her voice frantic.

He smiled and laughed, dropping to his knees. "Yeah, I... I'm okay. Are—are you safe? Are you hurt?"

"I'm so scared right now. I have no idea what's happening. Where are you?" she asked desperately.

A wave of comfort and responsibility to calm her washed over him. Nothing else mattered. *Why am I smiling?*

"Lucia, just... just listen to me. Everything is gonna be okay. I just need you to do something... promise me. Close your eyes."

He looked down the narrow path where the last traces of light remained with the rising sun, thankful they both existed in this exact cluster of seconds—privately between the ebony walls. The sun was joined by a partner directly above the skyline. The moon hung wet and slender, and he let himself pretend it was smiling back. He closed his eyes.

"What? Please, just tell me where you are!" she pleaded, her voice trembling.

"Just close your eyes and know that... know that I'm going to find you. Just keep them closed, please. Lucia? Lucia, are you—"

His eyes remained shut. She went first. The peach-colored hue of the rising sun, as its rays pierced through his closed eyelids, darkened. His world turned to black.

Chapter Twelve

A First Encounter

He felt the past flood back as he stood on the marble of the Curtis Center. The stone held the day's chill; arched windows caught the park's lights. A small speaker in the lobby corner played the last bars of The Cure's *Just Like Heaven. I opened up my eyes… alone above the raging sea.* It struck the same chord in him as always.

The building he remembered, nestled in the heart of Philadelphia, stood as a stately emblem of architectural grace. Its portico exuded timeless elegance. The stone exterior glowed eagerly under the shifting light, from the soft blush of morning to the gilded hues of dusk. Tall, curved openings punctuated the building's grandeur, reflecting the bustling energy of Washington Square Park just across the street. Framing the entrance, sturdy columns rose like protectors, inviting visitors into a world where history and artistry intertwined.

He raised his hands—smooth, unscarred. The window reflected a clean-shaven face he hadn't worn in years; even his knees felt light. This was the night he met her.

He stepped outdoors into the invigorating night air. The sounds of the evening—the distant whirr of traffic and the sporadic laughter of passersby—filled the metropolis. Though everything was the same as before, it all seemed more emotional, more genuine. He had to stop himself from dwelling on how long it had been.

Memories surfaced as he walked, each one bringing him closer to the beginning. He stepped forward but startled and quickly retreated as a SEPTA bus sped past, flinging gray, mushy snow from the street slightly into the air, scattering it onto the sidewalk. He made his way to the corner, recalling what was proper, waited for the light to turn green and crossed the street with purposeful yet light steps before entering the park grounds.

The park was a serene oasis where time seemed to linger gently. It unfolded like a verdant poem, its wide pathways shaded by ancient sycamores and elms, forming a cathedral of green covered in freshly fallen snow. In spring, he remembered how a riot of blossoms painted the air with soft hues, while autumn would set the leaves ablaze with gold and crimson, whispering accounts of seasons past.

The centerpiece, reading *Tomb of the Unknown Revolutionary War Soldier*, stood solemnly beneath the eternal gaze of a bronze George Washington, a trustworthy scout guarding the memories of those who fought for liberty. The flame nearby flickered perpetually, its glow softening the evening shadows—a testament to sacrifice and endurance. The fountain in the square's embrace, turned off until spring, would normally murmur its timeless melody, creating a sanctuary of peace amidst the city's vibrant pulse.

The air was crisp against his cheeks; inches of snow blanketed the ground, crunching gently beneath each step. He could see the bench in the distance—the same one she always sat on, engrossed in whatever book had caught her fancy that day.

Closer and closer, his heart began to race, the familiar sight opening before him with a clarity that made his chest tighten. Though it was a wintery scene, an intense warmth overtook him as he approached.

She sat on the bench, her breath visible in the chilly air, a long scarf spiraling around her neck. A slight smile curled her lips at something she had read, her focus absorbed in the book in her hands. Even before he met her, he had always smiled at that image.

Beneath winter's hushed embrace, a lamppost stood over her, a guardian of calm hospitality in the icy stillness. Its yellowish-brown glow spilled like liquid honey, pooling softly on the snow-draped ground, where each flake glistened like a shard of starlight. The crystalline air carried light in shimmering threads, weaving a cocoon of gentle radiance that defied the biting cold. Shadows of bare branches etched delicate lace across the illuminated frost, while the surrounding darkness seemed drawn to this fragile ember of coziness.

He stopped and stood directly in front of her, the lamplight casting his shadow over her, darkening the pages of her hardcover. He took a deep breath and spoke for the first time in ages. "So, it might be a sore subject, but... I remember all the names of your newts now."

Lucia looked up, her expression quickly shifting to painful bliss. She blinked hard and lifted her chin—an invitation to pretend this was only now. He could follow that.

She let out a breath, glanced down at the snowy ground, then back at him. "Not sure how much time we've got. Is that how you want to start?" She closed her book and gave him her full attention, a half-smile curling her lips, her eyes growing shinier.

"Okay, here goes. Wayne NEWTon, Olivia NEWTon John... and Figgy," he said, starting to break.

A long, wonderful pause ensued. The breeze began to blow cooler again, and the lamppost's illumination clicked on and off for a second.

"Impressive," she replied, a tear finally falling down her right cheek. A comfortable silence lingered, interrupted only by the frosty wind.

"I'm so glad I got to see you one more time," she said.

"There might be a next time," he replied, breath fogging his hands. "Please—let there be a next time. But... just in case—"

The bitter cold returned. He breathed into his palms to warm them. The thin moon hung clear above.

"Goodbye," she said, a last tear caught at the corner of her eye. The lamp flickered as a colder wind slipped through the trees.

He smiled back. "Goodbye."

About the Author

Patrick J. Williams is an emerging voice in literary fiction, combining vivid storytelling with themes of humanity's deepest struggles. Inspired by the relatable fears and excitement of new stages in life; including the graduation from the protected world of college and being thrust into the unknown, combined with heartbreak and a yearning for purpose, Patrick brings a fresh perspective to stories that bridge the gap between the real and the extraordinary. A Revelation is his debut novel, highlighting his talent for crafting emotionally resonant and thematically rich narratives.

Previous published work includes Soup Attempt for the Soul in Thanksgiving Tales: True Stories of the Holiday in America, Brian D. Jaffe, 2010; and God on Trial in Where the Mind Dwells, Eber & Wein Publishing.